breakaway

breakaway

ANDREA MONTALBANO

Philomel Books

An Imprint of Penguin Group (USA) Inc.

PHILOMEL BOOKS

A division of Penguin Young Readers Group.

Published by The Penguin Group.

Penguin Group (USA) Inc., 375 Hudson Street, New York, NY 10014, U.S.A.

Penguin Group (Canada), 90 Eglinton Avenue East, Suite 700, Toronto,
Ontario M4P 2Y3, Canada (a division of Pearson Penguin Canada Inc.).

Penguin Books Ltd, 80 Strand, London WC2R 0RL, England.

Penguin Ireland, 25 St. Stephen's Green, Dublin 2, Ireland
(a division of Penguin Books Ltd).

Penguin Group (Australia), 250 Camberwell Road, Camberwell,
Victoria 3124, Australia (a division of Pearson Australia Group Pty Ltd).

Penguin Books India Pvt Ltd, 11 Community Centre, Panchsheel Park,
New Delhi—110 017, India.

Penguin Group (NZ), 67 Apollo Drive, Rosedale, North Shore 0632, New Zealand
(a division of Pearson New Zealand Ltd).

Penguin Books (South Africa) (Pty) Ltd, 24 Sturdee Avenue, Rosebank,
Johannesburg 2196, South Africa.

Penguin Books Ltd, Registered Offices: 80 Strand, London WC2R 0RL, England.

Published simultaneously in Canada. Printed in the United States of America.

Design by Katrina Damkoehler. Text set in ITC Century.

Library of Congress Cataloging-in-Publication Data
Montalbano, Andrea.
Breakaway / Andrea Montalbano.   p. cm.
Summary: When seventh-grade soccer star LJ befriends Tabitha, who could not be
more different from her, LJ learns to curb her competitive nature, which has been
slowly alienating her friends. [1. Teamwork (Sports)—Fiction.   2. Soccer—Fiction.
3. Family life—Fiction.]   I. Title.
PZ7.M76342Br 2010   [Fic]—dc22
2009027035

ISBN 978-0-399-25215-0
10   9   8   7   6   5   4   3   2   1

To my children, Lily and William, who color my world.
And to my husband, Diron, for everything.

chapter 1

It's not easy to find your place in the world, especially when you're a kid.

Lily James knew that well: she was twelve now, and it had taken her a whole ten years to find *her* place. Ten years is a decade, one-tenth of a century, to be exact, and a century is, no doubt, a super-long time.

In case you're wondering, her place in the world isn't the sanctuary of her purple and red bedroom, or in Mrs. Krugman's seventh-grade English class, or even in the secret nook of her excellent tree fort: it's where she feels as comfortable as her old sneakers, as safe as under her comfy blanket and best of all, like a star.

Her place was on the soccer field. Any soccer field.

Lily James loved everything about it.

She lived to run, she ached to kick and she adored tackling, legally, of course, and never from behind. She thrilled at the pounding of her heart as she sprinted toward the goal, the black and white ball floating in front and the wind rushing past her ears, created solely by the movement of her own pumping arms and legs. She adored the smell of the grass and the fall colors in the trees all around, waving and falling like a million crazed fans. Soccer made her feel alive and important, because best of all, she could play.

In fact, if she were allowed to play soccer all day long, that's all she would do. She couldn't—school and sleeping and eating got in the way, and the winter made it tough. But other than that, the field was her place, the ball was her friend and soccer was her game.

It was hard to believe that she played her first real game for the Brookville Bombers Travel Team just two years ago. She could still remember the tingly feeling in her gut in the seconds before the referee, Mr. White, blew the whistle that very first game. A magical tension hung in the air—every girl had stood staring at the ball—just waiting. Waiting for the sound that would release them. At least that's how it felt to Lily that very first time. She'd eyed the regulation size 4 ball and in that leather orb she'd found herself and her special place.

Two years later, Lily was more experienced, but the wondrous anticipation remained the same. So far, this year's season had been incredible. Her team was 6–0, and on track to become league champions. Lily could still feel the bitter bite of last year's defeat in the finals. This year, she would settle for nothing less than the sweet taste of victory.

But trouble was coming before the morning's game even started: the referee was a father from the opposing team. That was never good news. Lily eyed him suspiciously but quickly put her gaze on the ball when she saw him draw a breath. She studied Maggie McNulty, the Riderdale Red Rockets' striker, who was resting her foot in a haughty way, making Lily wonder what was going on in that ponytailed head of hers. Would she go forward and attack, or would she pass the ball back to the center midfielder to blast upfield?

Lily's best friend, Vee Merino, was perched on the other side of the field's center circle, ready to pounce. She moved her head imperceptibly, and Lily nodded back. Vee was fearless, and Lily loved that about her. Even though she was pretty small compared to the rest of the players, when it came to Vee, size didn't matter. She was all courage. The ref finally exhaled and the whistle sounded in a sharp beep. The game was on.

Maggie tapped the ball to her teammate, who was immediately chased down by a dark-haired girl in a navy blue and yellow Bombers uniform. Vee the Bee. Buzzing in. The girl with the ball, a redhead with fair skin and a startled expression, looked around for a Rocket. No one was open. Flustered, she dribbled blindly for a moment as Vee pressed her attack. Then, turning around, she did the smart thing and passed the ball back to her own side of the field.

The center midfielder was a beefy girl, and Lily

knew she had a wicked right foot. Beefy girl made contact, but Lily could tell by the slapping sound that she'd hit it all wrong. Instead of going downfield, the ball went almost straight up like a firework. Lily looked up and saw it wobbling above in a crooked spin, the black and white squares blurring into gray. A girl from the other team stood close, jumping uselessly while Lily waited patiently, sure the ball would come to her.

That's just how it was with Lily and soccer. She knew that ball would come to her, and she knew what to do with it when she got it. Off the field she was a regular kid with homework and hang-ups, but on the pitch, she was a soccer magician. Her parents told her she started to kick the very same day she started walking. Her mom liked to point to her belly and say it started even way before that. Any chance she got, Lily had a ball. Some talents were from practicing all the time, but anyone who ever saw Lily play could tell it was the thing she was born to do.

The ball descended. The Red Rocket tried to shoulder Lily out of the way, but she stood her ground, protecting her position, and when the ball arrived, she lifted her foot ever so slightly. Catching it tenderly on her laces, she was off like a shot before it ever hit the ground. She moved right to avoid the midfielder and then heard a shout from the left.

"LJ! I'm open!"

Lily knew it was Vee calling. She lifted her head for a second and spied her friend making a run down the left. Using her right foot, Lily lifted a pass over another player. Vee trapped the ball and took off toward the goal.

"Get her!" Lily heard Maggie cry. "She's almost in the box!"

Lily didn't stop to watch but kept running full speed ahead, trying to find an open space to give Vee an option. Two other blue and yellow uniforms were speeding along the sides of the fields, and the red team was in shock. They weren't ready for this quick attack.

"Cross, Vee!" Lily cried as she charged across the eighteen-yard line—the penalty box. Anyone tripped by the defense in the box got a penalty kick. Just you and the goalie—one whistle, one shot.

Lily called again and Vee delivered a beautiful waist-high pass. Lily trapped the ball with her thigh and turned to shoot, but something caught her foot, and instead of making contact she fell straight to the ground, getting a mouth full of dirt.

She waited for the whistle but instead heard the referee shout, "Play on!"

Play on? Lily couldn't believe it. She had been tripped. She was about to score! Instead of getting a penalty kick, the game went on and she was left face-first on the ground tasting earthworm grit. She could hear her coach going ballistic.

"Hey!" Lily yelled, spitting out the mud. "Psssahk!! She tripped me!"

The red team goalie had the ball now and was about to launch it back upfield. Lily saw her smirk.

"Ref!" Lily yelled again. She deserved that penalty kick. She was the team expert and had already won two games on PKs this season. A fair call would basically guarantee her team a goal.

But the referee boomed, "Another word out of you and I'll give you a yellow!" Lily bit her lip and brushed herself off. Arguing with the man in black was a serious no-no. Two yellow cards and you were out of the game for good. Vee trotted over and helped Lily up.

"You okay?" she asked. "Keep your cool, LJ."

"I'm tryin'," Lily said, taking a deep breath. She wiped her mouth on her undershirt. "We should have scored."

"Don't worry, LJ, we'll get 'em."

Lily heard her coach hollering from the sidelines, "Get back in the game, LJ!"

The goalie punted upfield. Lily was convinced a terrible injustice had occurred, but there was nothing she could do about it. She knew her coach, Chris, was right: she had to get back into the game. She couldn't let her temper get the best of her again. Lifting her head, Lily jogged back toward her own goal, unable to shake off the feeling she'd just been robbed.

The rest of the first half was just as frustrating. Lily and Vee both had a few chances to score but missed by mere inches. One shot bounced off the crossbar and the Red Rockets' tall goalie grabbed the rebound at the last possible second. The other team turned out to be better than Lily had first thought. They went after every equally contested "50-50" ball like it was already theirs. Then Maggie nearly scored on a corner kick and the big midfielder could shoot—boom—from about forty yards away.

At halftime, Lily and Vee sucked on oranges and drank cold Gatorade as their coach started his pep talk.

"You guys are playing well, but you're getting beaten to the ball," Chris said to the group of sweaty girls gathered around.

"That referee is a cheater!" Lily interrupted.

"LJ, you need to snap out of it," Chris said immediately. "So you got tripped. Get used to it. They're marking you tighter than ever. You have to be bigger than that."

Lily studied her coach, weighing his words. Chris was pretty old—like thirty. He had long brown hair he wore tucked behind his ears and was cute in a droopy kind of way. He was really tall and skinny and tended to slouch over to make himself shorter.

Lily respected her coach. He knew a lot about soccer and had even played in college. He'd dreamed of playing professionally but told Lily his limbs were just the wrong dimensions. He'd blown out his knee and now he couldn't play soccer at all. Lily couldn't imagine anything as terrible as that.

"Lily, listen," he said, softer now. "We're better than they are. Cheating is not going to change that. We can beat them even if they *do* cheat. But we can't do that until you get your head back into the game. You missed some really good chances because you were too busy being mad at the referee. You're the captain of this team—we take our cues from you."

Lily nodded. He was right. "Yes, Coach."

"Good girl. Now let's go!"

The referee called the teams back to the field and the Bombers formed a huddle with all their hands piled high in the middle. Vee's was right on top of Lily's.

"On three," Chris said. "One, two, three!"

The girls all put their heads together and started a deep hum, excitement growing every second. The buzzing was low at first, like a faraway engine, but quickly grew louder and stronger, like a swarm invading the field. Lily nodded and suddenly all sixteen girls exploded, "Bombers Bombers Bombers . . . let's do it!"

They broke huddle and jogged back onto the field, Lily stepping gingerly over the white sideline, her most serious superstition. She was convinced touching the chalk coming on or off the field was terrible bad luck. She and Vee took their spots at center field, and since the Rockets got to kick off in the first half, it was the Bombers who got the ball this time.

"You ready?" Vee asked.

"Oh yeah," Lily said. "Chris wants us to drop it back to Avery and make a run down the right."

"Got it," Vee said as Lily gave a nod to Avery, the right halfback. Lily and Vee were the center forwards, and it was their job to play mostly offense. Avery was a halfback, and she played in the middle of the field on the right side—both offense and defense.

Lily adjusted her shin guards and retied her shoes. The referee checked to make sure both the goalies were ready and blew the whistle. Lily tapped the ball to Vee, who passed it back to Avery, and they both took off down the right-field line.

"Send me, Avery!" Lily cried. Right on cue a long pass zoomed down the line and Lily carried the ball at a sprint to the corner, moving past two red defenders in a blur. Vee dropped in right behind her.

"LJ!" she said in a tight bark.

Without even looking, Lily passed the ball back and made a run toward the near goalpost. Sara was the Bombers' left wing, who played offense on the other side, and she was yelling her head off.

"I'm open! I'm open!"

Suddenly a Rockets defender shoved Vee from behind, knocking her flat and stealing the ball.

Lily heard Vee hit the ground. Again she waited for the whistle, and again all the referee said was, "Play on!"

Lily wanted to yell, she wanted to argue, but she remembered Chris's words: *"We're better than they are. We can beat them even if they cheat."* Lily could see tough little Vee getting right up, so she charged to challenge the cheater with the ball. The red team player sneered at her and sprinted upfield.

Lily's anger was growing by the second. She was not going to let them get away with this.

Yet her chance to get even would have to wait.

During the rest of the second half, the teams went back and forth. Parents and fans heaved with every shot, but still no one scored until the Rockets were awarded a questionable free kick outside the box and found the back of the net.

Lily was deflated. The Bombers were facing their first loss of the season. Then with only five minutes left to play, little Vee led the charge. She raced downfield with the ball and connected with Amelia for a two-on-one and there was nothing the referee, or any of the Rockets, could do to prevent it. Amelia beat the tall goalie and scored. Now the game was tied.

Lily saw the referee looking at his watch. She knew they were running out of time. After a quick restart, the Bombers stole the ball back and there was a scramble at the top of the eighteen-yard box.

Lily felt a change: her anger was replaced with calm confidence. She could do this. Soccer justice would prevail.

Just then Maggie McNulty tripped over the ball as she was trying to kick it upfield. Avery, playing halfback, pounced on the loose ball and two Rocket defenders knocked into each other, falling to the ground and leaving the ball unmanned in the box. Both teams started screaming, "Loose ball! Loose ball in the box!!"

Lily was only steps away.

Out of the corner of her eye, she saw the goalie leave her line and heard her call, "Keeper's ball!"

Not if Lily could help it. She pushed her legs hard, keeping her eyes on nothing but the ball. She barreled ahead and beat the goalie by less than a second, taking control of the ball. The goal was open. She had the shot. As she wound up to take it, she felt someone grabbing her shirt.

She was getting pulled down from behind again!

This time she wasn't going to wait for any whistle because she knew it wasn't coming. Instead, Lily focused on the ball, rolling slowly across the face of the goal. She pulled herself forward with all her strength but couldn't hold herself up any longer. As she fell to the ground, she threw her legs forward and managed to slide along the grass as the goalie dove for the ball. She braced herself for the collision but kept reaching with her foot. Stretching as far as she could, she pointed like a ballerina, tapping the ball ever so slightly with the tip of her toe. Her touch was just enough to change its direction, and Lily watched as the ball slipped slowly under the looming goalie's black jersey.

The girl yelled in defeat and toppled on top of Lily, blocking her view and knocking the wind out of her. Lily couldn't see but heard the crowd start to roar.

It felt as if the ball took an hour to cross the goal line, but as Lily fought to catch her breath, she was finally rewarded with the unmistakably sweet beep of the referee's whistle.

Blue Bombers, 2, Cheaters, 1.

Vee ran over and pulled Lily to her feet, and the two friends jumped and hugged as their teammates and families celebrated.

Man, she loved this game.

chapter 2

The James family sat in rapt attention as Lily recalled the Bombers victory once again. That is, everyone except her little brother, Billy, who was busy constructing a garbanzo bean catapult.

"How many times are you going to tell that stupid story anyway?" he said from across the table.

"Hush now, baby," their mother, Toni, said, patting his hand, oblivious to the weapon aimed at her only daughter. Billy smiled sweetly at his mom, then turned and stuck his tongue out at Lily. Her mother absently stroked Billy's fire-red hair as he pulled back the thick green rubber band, lacing it through the tines of his dinner fork.

"How did you manage not to get run over by that goalie, sweetie?" her mom asked.

"I slid the ball right under her arm and ducked

out of the way," Lily answered quickly, hoping to defuse the worry on her mother's brow.

"You could have gotten kicked in the face!" her mother exclaimed. "You could have wound up with a serious concussion!"

"Oh, she's fine, Toni," Lily's father piped in from the kitchen. "Don't get started."

Lily smiled gratefully at her dad and nodded quickly to her mom, hoping she would stay calm. Most of the time, her mother was the best. She loved soccer and had even played a little in high school. Lily thought her mom had the world's coolest job, an entomologist (an insect specialist), and when she wasn't working, she spent all her time being supermom. She cooked, she played, she took her kids places and was overall a lot of fun.

There were only two small mom issues. First, being a bug scientist and one of the world's foremost experts on butterflies meant that her mom traveled a lot. Sometimes it felt to Lily that her mom was gone more than she was home. She would get emergency calls when the American snout butterfly swarmed parts of Texas or when a colony of rare silver-studded blues re-established themselves in a barn in Costa Rica. Her full name was Dr. Antonia Evangelista-James, and she made nature documentaries. Her friends and family called her Toni, but to most everyone else she was Madame Butterfly. She had an interactive website and a butterfly blog and even got on TV once in a while.

The second problem was bigger than the first. Lily's mom was bit neurotic, particularly when it came to her two kids. She seemed to over-worry about everything. Lily was convinced this was because she had to leave for weeks at a time, so when she was home, she would jam-pack her love and worrying into a few fretful days. She made everyday molehills into catastrophic mountains. A cold was certainly pneumonia, a slightly twisted ankle needed a full twenty-four-hour regimen of the RICE treatment (rest, ice, compression, elevation), and a piece of dirt in an eye was conjunctivitis or, worse, a rare infection brought back from the Amazon. Since her mom was actually trained to live in the jungle, she knew how to self-treat most medical problems and loved to demonstrate her skills on her two favorite victims, Lily and Billy. Lily sometimes enjoyed the extra attention, but most of the time it was safer to just keep Mom calm. She and Billy shared a healthy F.O.M. (fear of Mom). "Sniffle at your own risk," her brother liked to say.

"I think I see a little bruise under your eye," her mother whispered ominously now, getting up from her chair. "Let me take a closer look."

"Oh yeah, definitely, Mom. It's way swollen," Billy piped up.

Dad, Lily's hero, tried again. "Sweetie, she's fine."

"That goalie didn't touch me," Lily offered, even though that wasn't completely true. As usual, neither of her parents was at the game, a fact of life Lily had learned to live with, or at least pretended to.

"That was the game-winning goal, wasn't it, LJ?" her father asked. "Wish I could have seen it."

"Yeah!" Lily answered, relieved to see her mother sit back down but still staring at her closely. "There were like three hundred camcorders there. I'll ask Reese's dad."

"Terrific idea!" her father said a little too loudly, giving Lily a conspiratorial wink. He turned to his wife. "So shouldn't Pop Pop and Dina be here already? Hope their car didn't die again."

"Oh, you're right, Liam," Lily's mom said, looking up at the clock. "They should be here by now. Let me go call." Toni rushed to grab the kitchen phone. Lily relaxed and gave her dad a grateful smile. Worry transferred. Subject changed. Mission accomplished.

Pop Pop and Dina were Mom's father and sister. They came to dinner every Sunday, rain or shine. It was a James family tradition and pretty much went the same way every week: Dad cooked something great, Billy looked for trouble, Pop Pop looked for food and Dina complained about having to take care of Pop Pop. Dina was Mom's younger sister and not married. One night when she was supposed to be in bed, Lily overheard Dina saying she couldn't meet anyone because she lived with an old man, but most of the family agreed Dina was still single because she was kind of rough around the edges. She was pretty okay looking, in Lily's opinion, but had a bad habit of barreling over everyone and everything. She hardly ever said nice things like "sweetie," "honey" or "pumpkin," like Lily's mom did, and you could hear her coming from three rooms away because she never walked: she stomped like she'd filled her boots with concrete blocks. Lily knew Aunt Dina was sweet on the inside, but somewhere along the way she seemed to have grown tough on the outside, like she had personality bark.

As if on cue, a pair of headlights pulled into the driveway.

"They're here!" Lily yelled, pointing out the window as a small sticky missile smashed into her hair.

"Ouch!" she cried. She looked across the table to see her brother reloading.

"Is it your face?" her mother asked, rushing back into the dining room.

"No, it's Billy, he's shooting *ceci* beans again!"

"Billy, love, please don't shoot your sister," her mother said placidly, heading to open the front door. Imaginary wounds were always a crisis, but real projectiles were nothing. Billy was eight going on intolerable. If Lily said, "Don't put your foot on my chair," he would put his toe. If she told him not to come into her room, he'd reach an arm over the doorway claiming he wasn't technically "in" her room at all. Lily ducked as her brother shot another bean across the table but laughed when this one bounced off her head and landed in the lamp fixture above the table. Sometimes Billy was pretty funny, actually.

With a thud the front door flew open and Dina came charging into the dining room, dropping her jacket on the floor and plopping a pair of dirty wet gloves on the table.

"Hey, squirt," she said, sitting down with a clunk. "How 'bout a little vino?"

"I'll get it!" Billy said, jumping up from the table. Billy adored his unusual auntie.

"Sorry we're late," she said, wiping her nose on the back of her sleeve. "Old man lost his dentures again and the darn car wouldn't start. Such a piece of junk. I fixed it, though. So, Miss Beckham, how was the game yesterday?"

As Lily happily recalled the victory, Pop Pop shuffled in, grunting as he took his place at the end of the table.

"Hi, Pop Pop," she offered.

"Brutta."

That was the standard grandfather greeting. Lily knew that in Italian *brutta* meant "ugly," which was really her grandfather's way of saying she was pretty. It was an old Sicilian fear that if you talked too much about the beauty of a child, particularly a girl child, then the gods would come and take her away. So just to be safe, every time he saw her, he would call her ugly. Lily wasn't sure if she was pretty or not, but every time she was greeted by the word *brutta*, her shoulders involuntarily sagged just a little.

As usual, Pop Pop failed to notice the look on Lily's face, seeing only his empty plate. He was the kind of old man who demanded to know what was for dinner before lunch was even over. He'd lived too long to wait for anything anymore.

"What? No food?" he asked gruffly, conveniently forgetting he was the one who was late.

And so another James family dinner was

launched. Her dad had made something incredible as usual, which was no surprise since he was a chef who ran his own restaurant in town. He placed the food on the table just in time to stave off a meltdown from her grandfather. Tonight, it was chicken *scaloppine*, one of Lily's favorites. Lightly floured chicken sautéed in a tangy lemon sauce with olives and capers over spaghetti. A rare silence fell over the table as everyone dug in.

In celebration of Lily's goal, her dad brought out a giant *tartufo* for dessert, a beautiful dark mound of ice cream with nuts and fruit in the center, covered in chocolate. Lily looked around the table at her family and felt happy inside.

Her dad was smiling, her mom was home and had stopped looking worried and Lily had scored the game winner. She thought it was one of the best dinners they ever had, except of course when the garbanzo bean in the lamp started smoking and set off the fire alarm and Billy got sent to his room. Actually, Lily sort of enjoyed that part too.

chapter 3

A curious thing happened to Lily that Monday at Brookville Junior High. A few curious things, actually. For starters, lots of kids she didn't really know or who usually pretended not to know her were suddenly offering high fives.

"Way to go, LJ!" she heard at least three times, once in the hallway and twice in the middle of a heated dodgeball game. Next, instead of the football team scores, the principal, Ms. Sawyer, congratulated the team on their victory and even mentioned Lily's game-winning goal during assembly and over the loudspeaker. Then, to top it off, Tabitha Gordon passed Lily a note during social studies asking if she wanted to come over after practice. Tabitha Gordon was by far the most popular girl in the seventh grade. She played left fullback on the Blue Bombers, if you considered flouncing and falling as playing. Tabitha was slim and pretty in a Hannah Montana kind of way and was by far the richest kid in Brookville.

Lily James wasn't popular, and her family was most definitely not rich. Her mom and dad worked constantly and were always fretting about money. Recently, when Lily complained she didn't have an iPhone, or any cell phone, for that matter, her mother sat her down and told her they just couldn't afford the things that other kids in her wealthy town could. She'd explained to Lily, more than once over the years, that she and Lily's father had decided as a couple to follow their passions, butterflies and food, even if it meant always having to scrimp and save.

"Do what you love, and you will always feel complete," her mother advised. "With or without an iPhone."

Lily felt most complete when she was playing soccer and figured her mom might actually know a little something about life. But when Lily wasn't on the field, she just felt average. She was the third-tallest girl in her class, which gave her about three inches on most of the boys, who hadn't caught up on the whole growing thing just yet. Her hair was a mix of dark blond and strawberry, and she liked to keep it long. She usually wore a ponytail down her back or two braids, and during games one braid would occasionally whip around and smack her in the face. She liked to envision them as a distraction to her opponents. She had a gaggle of freckles on her nose which she kept track of in her bathroom mirror— sixteen at last count—but Lily thought her best feature by far was her eyes. They were a mix of green, blue and a slight yellowish-brown in the center. Technically, they were hazel. Her father called them "calico kitty eyes" and claimed to know how she was feeling by which color was dominant. Green when she was happy. Dark and stormy like a cyclone when she was mad.

Her mom said she was a fabulous mix of her dad's Irish and her mom's Italian blood. A perfect mutt. Lily wasn't sure she liked canine comparisons of any kind but figured since it was Mom talking there was likely a compliment in there somewhere.

When it came to the whole popularity business, Lily calculated she fell smack in the middle of the cool range. She wasn't *un*popular or a total dork, like poor picked-on Milo van Leerden. Rumor had it he tried to read every Wikipedia entry and by the letter *K* had fried his eyes so badly he could no longer focus on anything that wasn't twelve inches from his face. When the mean seventh graders weren't ignoring him, they were stealing his glasses and tormenting him by holding up signs that read *Loser*, which, of course, he couldn't see. Lily was neither loser nor tormentor. But she certainly was not among the top-tier kids, like Tabitha Gordon, who suddenly wanted to be her friend.

Lily was thinking about this exciting new development as she weaved her way down Hill Post Road toward the center of town. Hefting her backpack—the thing must have weighed forty-seven pounds—she thought, yes, something certainly was different today. Sure, she'd played a good game that weekend, but it never dawned on her that scoring the winning goal would result in so much attention.

That had never happened before. She was one of the popular kids today—no doubt about it—and Lily had to admit she liked it.

A lot.

Caring what other people thought was new to Lily. For most of her life, she'd felt more than content in her little world, but recently, she was starting to see things differently. She was beginning to want all the things she never noticed she didn't have: cell phones, RipStiks and, despite what her mother said, iPhones too. The change wasn't going over too well at home: asking for pricey loot in the James house was inevitably met with frosty stares that would give polar bears shivers.

She spied her dad's red restaurant awning at the end of the block and picked up the pace a bit. She loved the white cursive lettering that spelled out *Katerina's* in long flowing letters and rolling the *r* in the name like a purring kitten, the way Vee taught her. Maybe the bag was only thirty-five pounds today. Popular goal scorers like her shouldn't have any trouble carrying a bag with only thirty-five pounds.

. . .

Lily trundled quickly into Katerina's, past the bar and the front dining area to the back office, adjacent to the kitchen. She cast off her heavy bag with a thud and heard a commotion coming from inside. Her dad and Tomás were at it again.

"You don't need to put lemon slices," Tomás said loudly, but with his thick accent and machine-gun delivery it came out more like, *"Ju dan need topud leymon slighcess."*

"Sí, Tomás, that way they know there's lemon in the sauce," her father argued, his voice louder in any regular conversation with Tomás than even his maddest moment at home. Food just got him fired up.

"Too fanzy."

"No, it's not too fancy," Liam said.

"Como quieras," Tomás answered with disgust, dumping the lemon into the sauté pan and walking away. "Iz jor cho."

Lily realized they were trying out recipes for tonight's dinner special. Spotting Lily, Tomás came over and gave her a big hug. *"Hola, muchacha. Tu padre . . .*" he said, then, trying to think of the word, knocked on his own head with his knuckles.

"Hardheaded?" Lily guessed, and Tomás laughed. "*Sí*! By de way, nice goal. *Muy linda.*"

"*Gracias,*" Lily answered, feeling instantly safe inside the warm kitchen. Tomás had been at the game over the weekend, but Lily's dad had had to work as usual. Tomás was Vee's father and her own dad's right-hand man. The two men argued like enemies but loved each other like brothers. Tomás ran the kitchen, took care of ordering all the food and sometimes cooked when her dad wasn't at the restaurant, which wasn't often. Saturday lunches and dinners were super-busy. When Lily complained once that her dad was the only father to miss all the games, he'd tried to explain that weekends alone made up about 30 percent of the business Katerina's did all week.

Most afternoons, when her mom was working, Lily came to the restaurant and did her homework in the little office or kicked the ball around in the back parking lot with Vee. They'd been best friends for as long as Lily could remember, playing while their fathers worked in the kitchen. This was the place she'd really learned to love soccer. She and Vee would practice their skills or play pickup with any willing waiter or busboy. After-school afternoons were a never-ending USA-Mexico mini World Cup where the makeshift goals might have been garbage cans, but the passes were magic.

Vee and Tomás lived in the next town over, so she went to a different school, but after much begging, Liam had cleared it so Vee could play on the town's travel team with Lily.

"Where's Vee?" Lily asked Tomás now.

"*Afuera, mi amor,* where else?" he said, pointing to the rear door.

Lily sighed as Tomás and Liam resumed their bickering, this time about pepper flakes.

"LJ, you need to get all your homework done before practice," her father called after her. "Be back in ten minutes."

"Okay," Lily answered with a smile, grabbing her ball and running out the door to the back steps.

Her father gave her ten minutes every day but always let her have an hour.

Lily spied her friend. "How many?"

"Twenty-eight!" Vee answered. "A new record!"

"Awesome!" Lily said, joining Vee on the concrete below. "Let me try."

The two girls juggled in silence, with only whispered counting as each tried to keep the soccer ball up in the air, using their thighs, feet, shoulders and heads. Occasionally, one or the other would shout out a number.

"Twenty-one!" from Vee.

"Twenty-nine!" Lily counted. "We're getting closer. I heard that Landon Donovan can do like a thousand. Let's try for fifty by the end of the week."

"Deal!" Vee answered, tapping the ball from thigh to thigh.

"So guess what?" Lily said.

"You got new cleats?"

"No, but I've got my eye on a Nike pair. So really, guess what?" Lily asked again.

"What?"

"At school today, they announced our win over the loudspeaker."

"Dude!" Vee shouted while trying to balance the ball on her forehead.

In Vee language "dude" was an acceptable form of expression for nearly every occasion. Happy, sad, impressed, as in right now, with the right tone all emotions could be conveyed with the appropriate usage of her friend's favorite word. Vee had not one hint of the accent her father carried from Mexico because she'd been born in New York, like Lily. Where Lily was tall, Vee was petite. Lily was blond, while Vee's hair was so black it sometimes resembled the violet hue of a blueberry. Her cocoa skin without a single freckle. Basically, she was a physical yin to Lily's yang. Vee's mom had died when Vee had been too young to remember, so it was just her and Tomás. To Lily, the two were like family, but better.

Lily was excited to tell Vee about the rest of her day. "And you won't believe this one. They announced that I scored the winning goal in assembly too."

"No way! Man, I should have been there!" Vee

said, and Lily wished for approximately the millionth time that they were in the same school.

"Let's see how many headers we can do together," Lily suggested. Vee kicked her ball to the side and Lily tossed hers in the air. Vee watched it come down and headed it back to Lily. Lily wondered if Tabitha's house had a pool table.

"Ouch!" Lily yelled as the ball glanced off her head and went flying. Vee turned to chase it down.

"The trick is to keep your eyes on the ball, remember?" Vee teased.

"I guess I'm a little distracted." Lily laughed. "It was a pretty cool day, I have to admit."

"You're a celebrity!" Vee cheered, tossing the ball back.

"Oh, and get this one," Lily said, mid-header. "Tabitha Gordon even asked me to come over to her house today after practice."

Vee caught the ball. "She did?"

"Can you believe that?"

"*The* Tabitha Gordon?"

"Yep."

"Are you gonna go?" Vee asked.

"I guess," Lily answered. Of course she was going.

"Isn't she the girl you said runs like Cinderella with one missing shoe?"

Lily smiled. "Yep."

"Well, I can't wait to hear all about this one," Vee said, picking up the other ball and heading inside.

Me either, thought Lily.

chapter 4

Lily raced to finish the last of her pre-algebra problems as Vee leaned against the wall with her arms crossed, packed and ready to go. Practice started in ten minutes. Vee hadn't said anything more about Tabitha's invitation, and Lily got the feeling it was probably better not to mention it again.

"Done!" Lily said, using her fingers to gather her work like she was raking a pile of leaves.

"I don't want to do any push-ups today!" Vee said. Both girls knew their coach's rule: ten push-ups for every five minutes of missed practice.

"Me either," Lily said. Vee held the door to the kitchen open so Lily could sprint through. With Vee trailing right behind, she ran through the bar and waved good-bye to her father. Lily charged ahead to the restaurant door and held it open for Vee. They were cutting it way too close today. Sunlight from the crisp fall day flooded the street as they ran together out onto the sidewalk. Lily let the door go, but before her eyes could adjust to the light, she heard the sound of a collision.

"Hey! Watch where you're going!" she heard a boy yell. Lily bolted onto the sidewalk to find an angry-looking Griffin Prescott IV lying in the middle of the street next to a stunned-looking Vee. She was rubbing her arm and Griff was holding his wrist. A shiny new BMX dirt bike was lying next to him in the street, and Lily could see the palms of his hands were scraped.

"What happened?" Lily asked.

"She ran right into me," Griffin said, pointing at Vee. "That's what happened."

"I'm sorry," Vee said immediately. "I didn't see you."

Vee went over and offered a Griffin a hand. "Are you okay?"

"Just do me a favor and leave me alone," he grunted, refusing Vee's outstretched arm.

"Really, I'm sorry," Vee said, backing away. Lily thought she looked like she was about to cry. Lily knew Griffin because his father had just opened a sports bar called Heritage, across the street, and because they went to the same junior high. She was not a fan. He was in eighth grade and quarterback of the Brookville Junior squad. At school, everyone just called him G-4. Going by your initials was one thing, in Lily's opinion, but sticking in digits was just too much.

Vee saw a car approaching and ran over to move the BMX. "I'll get your bike out of the street."

"Keep your hands off!" he warned.

"Hey, take it easy," Lily said. "She said she was sorry."

"*She* should stop being sorry and just watch where she's going."

Lily saw Vee's face begin to crumple. Lily felt bad that Griffin had hurt his hands, but he wouldn't let it go.

"*You're* the one who's always riding your bike on the sidewalk," Lily answered. "It wasn't like she did it on purpose."

"I didn't," Vee tried to explain. "We were rushing to practice."

"Figures," G-4 muttered under his breath.

"What's that supposed to mean?" Lily asked.

"You think getting your goal announced at school means you're something in this town? You have a lot to learn," Griffin said. Lily was confused at first, but then it finally registered: Brookville Junior football had gotten slaughtered in their last game 35–0. He was jealous the school had announced the travel soccer scores instead of the regular football results.

"Well, at least *we* win for Brookville," Vee said, straightening herself up.

"We?" Griffin Prescott said, picking up his bike. "That's a joke. You don't even live in this town, do you? You shouldn't even be playing for Brookville. Why don't you go back where you belong?"

Vee gasped, and Lily couldn't take any more. Before Griffin could say another word, Lily tossed her ball up and volleyed it directly at his head. It flew like a rocket, and he ducked just a millisecond before the ball would have hit him like a missile, stumbled to the ground and smacked his hands hard on the pavement again. The ball whizzed by and slammed into the big glass yellow *H* hanging in front of the Heritage sports bar. All three stopped to watch as the giant letter swung precariously back and forth.

"Dude!" Vee yelled.

Oh, please, don't let it fall, Lily prayed to herself.

"You are so busted," G-4 said.

Lily grabbed her ball as Vee turned her by the shoulders and pushed her down the street away from the tottering sign.

"LJ, let's *go*!"

Lily and Vee were more than ten minutes late for practice, and Chris wanted an explanation. He spotted them as he emerged from the team clubhouse with a stack of bright orange cones.

"Well?" he said, his green shirt and skinny arms making him resemble a loosely arranged bunch of beans. Before Lily could claim some excuse like babysitting, Vee blurted out everything about their run-in in town. Chris nodded with lanky understanding as long brown strands flopped across his forehead.

"Go warm up," he said. "We'll talk later."

Lily was so agitated when she and Vee started their practice circuit that her ten right-footed passes were more like smart bombs.

"Take it easy, LJ," Vee said. "You trying to take my head off too?"

"Sorry."

"I *am* the only one that goes to Lakewood," Vee said after a few more passes. "Everyone else on the team goes to Brookville Junior or St. Mary's."

"So what?" Lily answered. "Just because you live in a different town doesn't mean you can't be on the travel team. Don't let that jerk get to you. He's a loser and doesn't know what he's talking about."

Vee laughed. "That's ten," she said, making the last pass. "Now volleys. But don't kill me!"

Throwing the ball high into the air and watching it come down, Lily timed her kick after one bounce. She connected with the laces of her right foot and sent the ball sailing with a satisfying thump. Vee made an easy trap and sent it sailing back, at least thirty yards. But on the next volley, Vee caught the ball in her hands and said in a low voice, "You could get in a lot of trouble, LJ. You know Mr. Prescott is like on the board of everything in Brookville."

Lily shrugged. "The sign didn't break, right?"

Vee tossed the ball back. "It was a really nice shot." She giggled, obviously pleased LJ had come to her defense. "Did you see the look on his face?"

Lily nodded, and the two girls spent the rest of their warm-up circuit reliving the near pummeling of G-4. Chris made them do the same warm-up every practice: ten passes, ten half volleys, ten full volleys and then ten headers. On most days it was the perfect way to get their bodies ready to play and their minds away from homework, boys and gossip.

Chris blew the whistle and announced they would be working on three-v.-twos: three offenders trying to beat two defenders. Lily, Amelia and Vee would take on Riley, Sue, plus the goalie, Beth. Usually, Lily loved the drill because the offense had a one-person advantage. The girls made three lines at midfield. On her first run, Lily took the ball straight at the front defender, Riley, and at the last second passed it off to Amelia on her left. She sprinted straight behind in an overlapping run and got the ball back down by the end line. Vee was calling from the middle of the box, so Lily pulled the ball back with her right foot and put a cross in. It was way too high and sailed off the field and onto the street.

"Shoot," Lily muttered, stomping her feet and kicking a free ball off the field. She never missed a cross like that. Lily jogged to half field and got back in line.

"Hey, LJ, last time I checked, the goal was over there," Chris teased.

After a few more turns, her coach decided it was time to have a half-field scrimmage. He kept the girls divided into offense and defense. For Lily practice kept getting worse. She missed her passes, fumbled her traps and even tripped once on her untied laces. It seemed the harder she tried to concentrate, the worse she did. Her frustration level was on the rise, percolating into anger. It always started the same for her: a hot flash at the top of her neck that she could actually feel crash over her in a wave. Sometimes she could let it wash over her, take a deep breath and then regain control, but lately those dark and stormy eyes had been brewing regular tsunamis.

Lily took a deep breath now. She tied her shoes in double knots and sprinted back into the scrimmage. Reese and Vee connected on a pass down the line and crossed it right to Lily. Lily leapt to redirect the ball into the goal with her head but mistimed her jump. The ball glanced off the back of her head and flew over the crossbar. She snapped and fell to the ground in a first-class fit, pounding her fists into the ground with a frustrated yell.

Chris had seen enough. "LJ. Take five," he called. Lily sulked over to the water cooler.

A few minutes later Chris blew the whistle and the girls all gathered for break and what Chris liked to call "think time." Most of his talks focused on strategy, last week's game or the upcoming opponent. All sixteen players sat in a semicircle with Chris on his haunches in the middle. Lily was afraid to make eye contact.

"We've got a big match this weekend, girls," he

said. That was an understatement. Everyone knew they were playing Castle Creek, the best team in the league. The game was a must win if they wanted a shot at the championship.

"Castle Creek likes to take charge early and push hard. They're quick off the ball and their striker, Molly Barrelton, has a wicked banana kick. We've been doing really well up front, but we're going to have to keep the pressure up to move through their defense. I want us to work on some set pieces this week and, in case it's a tie, penalty kicks. Beth and Lily, I want you to alternate in goal."

Lily looked up. Goalie? She sometimes played backup goalie in practice, but in her mind, it had always been just for fun. She had to be on the field for Castle Creek. I'm a goal *scorer*, not a goal *stopper*, she thought. Plus, penalty kicks were her specialty. There was a secret to taking them, Lily had learned, but it took a lot of practice. Lily had never missed a penalty kick and didn't want to start now.

She looked up at her coach in disbelief, but Chris just kept right on talking.

"I also wanted to let you girls know that I got a call from the coach of the State Select Team. He's going to try and make the game." Chris paused for effect. "He's got his eyes on some of the local players."

Lily held her breath. All the best players were on the state team. Was the coach coming to see her?

"Who is he coming to scout?" Avery asked.

"He didn't say specifically," Chris answered, but his eyes darted quickly to Lily. "So everyone's got a shot. But we've all got to keep cool heads and think like a team. Remember we're there to win this game, first and foremost. This is not a tryout."

He starting pacing in the little cage created by the surrounding girls. "You know, soccer is as much a psychological game as it is a physical one. Now, it's my responsibility as your coach to teach you the right moves on the field, but it is also my responsibility to teach you how to think."

Lily had a feeling the comments were directed at her.

"The key to being a good soccer player is finding equilibrium," he said, holding both of his hands palm up, like he had an invisible baby in his arms.

"Equilibrium? Is that a skin lotion?" Tabitha Gordon asked with a perky grin. "I think my mom has a vial. It's got, like, fish eggs or something?"

Lily saw Vee roll her eyes, and Chris shook his head as if to clear cobwebs from his brain. "No, Tabitha, it's not a lotion. Equilibrium means to find balance. It means you have to learn to harness your emotions and, most of all, to think before you act. No matter what. For example, if we score a goal in the first five minutes of the game, we can't just run around freaking out like we've won the match. We've got to remember we have the rest of the game to play."

"Or, like, if we get scored on?" Susie, the eternal defender, asked.

"Exactly, Sue," Chris said. "If we get scored on, it doesn't mean we've lost the game. But if we exert our energy worrying about what has already happened, then we're losing the psychological game first, and then the real game will follow."

Chris started pacing faster, then stopped and locked eyes with Lily. "The key is to recognize that we all have emotions—positive and negative—but to keep them to a dull roar. To keep focused on what's important and block out what, or who, isn't."

Lily tilted her head to the side to listen, trying to ignore Tabitha Gordon's humming as she attempted to French braid loose threads on her blue socks.

"People who don't understand soccer—and there are *lots* of them—don't realize it's a thinkers' game. Soccer is really just a string of decisions. Do I pass? Do I go back? Or do I wait for them to make a mistake? At the end of the day, it will be the quality of those decisions that determines the outcome."

Lily could tell Chris was pleased with today's little speech because he rubbed his hands and twirled his whistle string in a big arc. Chris always twirled his whistle when he was happy.

"Okay, I want everyone to take a lap to loosen up and then I want offense at the top of the D and defense in a four-person wall."

The team got up as a group and started to jog around the field. "LJ, hang back for a second."

Lily stayed behind. "Coach?"

"Sit," Chris commanded.

She sat.

"You hear what I'm saying?"

She nodded.

"This select team coach? He did mention one player's name."

"Mine?" Lily asked.

"Yours," Chris said with a nod. "People are noticing you, LJ, but you have to remember to keep your cool. Part of what makes you such a great soccer player is your passion. But that temper of yours can hurt you. What you did in town today was stupid and impulsive, and how you acted at practice was immature. Who cares what some kid says? You could have hurt him. Or you could have broken that sign and gotten in a lot of trouble. Then you missed a cross. Big deal. I know you want to be a great soccer player, LJ, but you have to learn to think with your head, not just your heart."

Lily looked at the ground.

"LJ?"

"I heard you," Lily answered, tired of the lectures. "I'm not going to be playing goalie this weekend, am I? What if there's a penalty kick? How am I going to be the one to take it?"

"You'll be playing where the team needs you, LJ," he answered sharply. "Now give me thirty."

Lily stepped to the side of the field, jumped over the line and dropped to the ground. "All the way down," Chris said.

Lily toughed out ten push-ups.

"That's the regular twenty for being late and ten extra for acting like a prima donna during practice."

Lily strained as she lowered herself through ten more and saw some of her teammates watching. A hot flush filled her cheeks.

She puffed out the last ten.

"That's it for today, everyone," Chris announced finally. "Practice Wednesday. Okay, LJ, you're free."

Lily got up and looked for Vee, who was changing her shoes nearby. Lily was dying to get out of there.

"Ready, LJ?" It was Tabitha Gordon.

"For?" Lily said.

"You're coming over, right? And staying for dinner?"

Lily hesitated for an instant.

"Okay, whatev," Tabitha said, looking hurt.

Between the G-4 run-in, select team announcement and Professor Soccer Coach, Lily had forgotten Tabitha's invitation. "Tabitha, wait. I just need to check with my mom," she said, trying to recover.

"Call from your cell," Tabitha suggested.

"Uh, I left mine at home," Lily lied. Vee gave her a look but didn't say anything. Lily felt a funny pit in her stomach.

"Oh, I do that all the time," Tabitha said, handing her a sleek black iPhone. "Use mine."

"Awesome," Lily said, grabbing the cell.

"See ya, LJ," Vee said, slinging her bag over a shoulder.

"Bye!" Lily answered distractedly. She didn't even look up. She was too busy pretending she had a clue how to make the phone work.

chapter 5

"**It's all set,**" Lily said, handing back the iPhone. "My mom will pick me up at seven. I can't stay for dinner, though. She's got to go to L.A. in the morning."

"Cool!" Tabitha shrieked. "Is she in the biz?"

The biz? Lily had no idea what Tabitha was talking about.

"Uh, my mom is a bug expert."

"A what?"

"An entomologist. A lepidopterist, actually. You know, someone who studies butterflies."

"What's in Los Angeles? Celebrity bugs? I heard Zac Efron keeps crickets."

Oh, this is going to be a long afternoon, Lily thought. "She told me she has to go help arrest a Japanese butterfly smuggler at the airport."

"Seriously?"

"Yep."

"Wow" was all Tabitha said. Lily wished for what felt like the thousandth time that she could just tell people, "My mom's a nurse." She thought her mom's job was cool, but everything about her family seemed to require an explanation. She tried to think of a way to change the subject. Lily tied her shoes together and put on her backpack and headed for the gate.

"Where ya going?" Tabitha said.

"Uh, your *house*?"

"Oh, man, I am way too tired to walk up the hill. Where's Rini?" Tabitha looked around.

"Who's Rini?" Lily asked.

"My mom's driver. He's usually around here somewhere."

"Your mom doesn't know how to drive?"

"She knows how to drive." Tabitha laughed. "Drive me crazy, that is. Actually, Rini takes her places so she doesn't have to find a parking place. She's *very busy*."

A sleek black car pulled up. "Need a ride?"

"Hey, Rini," Tabitha said, opening the door. The tiny man driving the enormous car flashed a brilliant smile and the two girls piled in. His face lit up even more when Tabitha introduced Lily.

"Oh, miss, you are quite a player," Rini said. "Tabitha tells me all the time she wishes she could play like you."

"Really?" Lily asked, flattered and a little surprised. She was always under the impression soccer was an afterthought for Tabitha.

"Rini!" Tabitha yelled.

"Oh yes, you have quite a fan here," Rini continued, smiling.

Lily settled into the supple seat and thought maybe things were starting to look up. The drive up to the Hills took less than five minutes, but Lily was stunned at how different everything looked. The houses were more like small castles, with manicured lawns and elaborate gardens. Tabitha's house had a long winding driveway and an imposing wooden door with some kind of scary gargoyle knocker.

"Yeesh," Lily said, ducking as they passed inside. "Where'd you get that guy?"

"Oh, that's just some antique something or other one of the decorators found," Tabitha told her. "Gives me the creeps too. Makes me feel like my house is haunted."

A housekeeper named Marta was waiting with pizza snacks and soda when the girls arrived. Looking around the enormous and spotless kitchen, Lily imagined what her father would think. It was bigger than the kitchen at Katerina's. One difference she noticed right away: there wasn't any food to be seen. Every counter was bare. In her house, baskets overflowed with tomatoes and avocados, and battered spice racks hung permanently askew. Dried oregano flakes littered the floor like fall leaves and tickled Lily's bare feet. Lily admired the metal and glass but wondered if anyone actually cooked in this place.

"My father would kill for this kitchen," Lily said.

"My father would die if he stepped foot in this kitchen."

Both girls laughed.

"Well, your mom must be a great cook, then," Lily said.

"My mom's not too big on the whole food thing. I think she ate something, like, last fall."

An image of her mom scarfing down a big sloppy pizza flashed in Lily's mind. She couldn't imagine a mother who didn't like food. "Oh, man," Lily said, "she better stay out of our kitchen. Food is life in my house."

Lily suddenly realized she was starving and reached for another pizza snack.

"Would you like some more?" Marta asked, noticing Lily's appetite. "These are Tabby's favorite."

"Tabby?" Lily repeated while nodding a hearty yes to more.

"My kitten," Marta said, giving Tabitha a kiss on the top of her head. "I've been taking care of her and her brother since she was just a baby." Marta was a sweet-looking stout lady with dark hair who radiated the same sort of personal sunshine that Rini had. Lily was surprised to see Tabitha wolfing down the snacks and smiling. Lily was beginning to realize that the Tabitha at home was different from the ditzy, non-eating, Queen Tabitha from school.

"So, did you ask her?" Marta asked Tabitha.

"Marta!" Tabitha looked upset.

"Ask me what?" Lily wanted to know.

"Nothing, nothing."

"Really, what was it?"

"Come on, Tabby, ask her."

"Yeah, ask me."

Tabitha glared at Marta. "Want to see the game room?"

"Sure," Lily answered, confused. "That's what you wanted to ask me?"

Tabitha paused for a second and then added, "Yep, that was it."

chapter 6

It was close to six when they headed downstairs to the basement. Lily's eyes bulged out of her head when she saw how decked out the place was. There *was* a pool table. Also air hockey, an iPod docking station and two console chairs attached to the latest Wii technology. Every different kind of MP3 player and PSP was scattered on the massive coffee table. It was like living at Best Buy.

"Wow," Lily said, impressed. "All this stuff is yours?"

"Well, my brother and my dad are into the games and stuff. I mostly watch TV or movies down here."

Lily was scared to touch anything. Lush leather recliners were set up in front of a giant movie screen. "What's that smell?" she asked.

"Popcorn machine. Why? You want some?"

"No, thanks." Lily kept exploring. She caught her own reflection from the mirrors off the back wall. She noticed there was a long wooden railing set up for dancing.

"You do ballet?" Lily asked.

"A little," Tabitha said, walking quickly away and plopping down into a beanbag.

Lily did a floppy pirouette in the mirror. She looked more like a spastic panda than a prima ballerina.

"Let me try that again!" Lily said, lifting her arms above her head and giving her upper body a violent twist. She was in her socks from practice and immediately slipped to the floor in a comic pratfall. Tabitha grabbed her sides and gave a prolonged silent laugh. When she composed herself, she stood up and came over to the bar. "Here, let me show you."

Tabitha stood tall, pushed out her chest and executed a perfect pirouette that showed Lily she danced a lot more than "a little."

"You're really good!" Lily said, amazed that klutzy old Tabitha could be so graceful. On the soccer field, she was all knees.

"Hey, want to go kick around?" Tabitha asked casually. "I have a goal set up out back!"

"I'm really tired from all those drills and push-ups," said Lily, who was never really too tired for soccer. She just didn't want to leave this awesome game room.

"Oh, man, I hate those drills," Tabitha said.

"Tabitha, do you even like playing soccer?"

"Of course. Why?"

"Well, sometimes you look kind of bored out there."

"Bored?" Tabitha thought for a minute. "No, I'm not bored."

"Don't take this the wrong way, but I mean, if you tried a little harder and listened to Chris, you might get more playing time."

Tabitha shrugged. "I guess. But sometimes it's better not to try too hard."

Lily couldn't imagine not giving it her all. "How can you not try?"

"Well, if you don't really try, then you can't really fail, right?"

"I guess. I never thought about it like that."

Tabitha stood and looked in the mirror. She spoke aloud but seemed to be talking mostly to herself. "And if you don't fail, then no one can be too disappointed."

Lily wasn't sure how to respond, so she just counted freckles. Twenty-one. Five more. She looked over at Tabitha then and realized there might be a lot more going on in that blond head than she'd ever suspected.

Lily was a little uncomfortable in the silence but jumped when a sudden commotion erupted upstairs. "What's that?" she asked, concerned.

Tabitha listened and then shook her head. "That's just Mark, my brother."

"Wow, I thought *my* brother was loud."

"Oh, Mark and his friends think being loud is cool. And they're all about being cool."

"What do your mom and dad say?"

"Say? Nothing. Mark can do no wrong. He's Mr. Untouchable."

The commotion migrated. Laughter and yelling

came down the stairs in a thunderous gallop. Mark was first, followed by his two friends, all eighth graders Lily recognized from school. Mark glared at his sister as he took his throne in front of the Wii.

"Get out," he said immediately to Tabitha, then hit play. Grand Theft Auto blasted from what seemed like forty surround sound speakers.

"We were here first!" Tabitha shot back.

"We?" Mark pressed pause and spied Lily for the first time. "Who are you?"

"I'm Lily."

"Lily. Lily who?" Mark asked. He had a sneering grin that gave Lily the creeps.

"Lily James."

Mark looked unimpressed and turned back to the massive flat screen. The game resumed with blasts of gunfire and screaming.

"Lily James?" another voice boomed from behind.

Lily turned as someone else came down the stairs. She caught his eyes for just a second and immediately froze.

It was Griff. G-4. He looked at Lily, then back to Mark.

"What's she doing here?"

Everything went silent as Mark hit mute and his perpetual look of coolness flashed an instant of surprise.

"You know her?" he asked.

"Yeah, I know her," Griff answered in a grunt that clearly said he wished he didn't. He sauntered over to the second butterscotch-colored leather recliner and pressed resume. Lily thought she saw him rubbing his wrist. Screaming, shouting and mayhem from the TV screen filled the room. Mark looked amused. Lily wanted to run up the stairs.

He asked his sister, "What *is* she doing here?"

"She's on my soccer team."

Griff stayed focused on trying to spirit a virtual mafia boss to safety. Bombs exploded as he aimed his controller. Lily prayed they would stay interested in the game. No luck. Another of Mark's friends recognized her.

"Wait," Colin said. "I know who she is too. She's

the one who made the goal at the game yesterday. They announced it in assembly . . ."

Mark shrugged, clearly unimpressed.

Griff interrupted. "Try, she's the one who broke the sign at my dad's sports bar."

Mark nodded and gave Lily an approving look. "Now, *that* is impressive," he said.

Lily still hadn't moved or said a word. She was unable to speak. Her faced felt flushed and her palms had started to sweat. She wanted to defend herself, but for some reason, being in this room with these kids had rendered her mute. It was the complete opposite of how she felt on the field, where she was strong and confident. Now, being sized up by Mark, Griff and his friends, she felt two inches tall.

"I didn't break the sign" was all she managed to answer in a lame voice.

"Well, how did it break, then?" Griff answered.

Lily had no idea what he was talking about. When she last saw the sign, it was in perfect shape. Wobbling, but certainly intact.

"It didn't fall! And the ball never even touched you."

Griff shrugged. "Your dad will be getting the bill."

Griff turned back to the big screen, but Mark paused the game again.

"Wait a second. This *girl* kicked a ball at you?"

Mark's question got the attention of all the boys in the room, and Griff looked like he would rather rat on a mob boss than answer the question.

"No, man. She never touched me. Just forget it." Griff threw down the controller and headed up the stairs. "I'm outta here."

Mark laughed and followed G-4, stopping directly in front of Lily. Lily felt like all the air in the room had been sucked out. Her chest tightened, and she couldn't seem to get any oxygen in her lungs. It had seemed so cool to come and hang out with Tabitha at her fancy house. But maybe coming here was just a bad idea.

"Lily James, eh?" Mark repeated her name. "I'm keeping an eye on you."

chapter 7

"**So I still** don't get it. What's that supposed to mean, 'I'm keeping an eye on you'?" Vee asked, tossing a weathered rainbow hacky sack high into the air.

"No idea," Lily answered.

"And that was Queenie's brother?"

"Yeah, Mark," Lily answered. "Some kind of Malfoy wannabe."

Vee laughed and started bouncing the leather beanbag off Lily's bedroom wall. She was lying on her back on Lily's bed as autumn rain trickled down the windowpanes. It was the kind of dreary storm that kept the day dark and damp with just enough chill to make Chris cancel their Friday pre-game practice.

"What I'm worried about is my dad," Lily said as she laid out her uniform. "If he finds out, I'm hamburger."

"Hamburger?" Vee asked, catching the tiny leather beanbag.

"Hamburger," Lily said. "As in dead meat."

Vee chuckled and kept on throwing the hacky sack. "Maybe you should just tell your parents what happened."

"Are you kidding? They already think I need anger management. I'm going to just have to keep my fingers crossed that G-4 was bluffing." Lily knew already he wasn't bluffing about the sign being down. She'd checked the very next day, and sure enough, it was gone. But so far, no bill of any kind had arrived and no one had said anything else to her about it.

"I can't believe he was at Tabitha's house," Vee said.

"Me either. He walked right into the game room like he owned the place."

"Game room?" Vee caught the ball again.

"I told you, this place was so totally tricked out. It had everything: pool table, video games, dance floor . . . you should see it."

"Like that would ever happen," Vee said.

"What's that supposed to mean?"

"Oh, like the queen of Brookville would ever have a Lakewood loser like me over to her house."

"Don't say that, Vee. She might."

"Yeah, right. So does Miss Thing shake her stuff down there?"

Lily walked over to the window and looked at the gloomy sky. She was dying to tell Vee all about the ballet bar and Tabitha's beautiful dancing, but she heard that tone again and hesitated. Tabitha had admitted to Lily she didn't really want to dance at all anymore. Her parents had started her when she was three, and she was sick of the never-ending lessons in her basement. When she told her parents she wanted to try something new, her father initially said no. "Team sports are for boys," he'd told her. The only way Tabitha was even allowed to play soccer was to promise her dad she'd stick with ballet.

Lily looked over at Vee and decided to change the subject. "This rain better stop soon," she said.

"I like playing in the rain," Vee said. "*Mucho* mud equals *mucho* sliding."

"Yeah, me too," Lily said. "But not against Castle

Creek. They're too fast and too good. Anything can happen in the rain."

"Are you going to have to play goalie?" Vee asked.

"Me? No way. I'm a striker. Plus, this game is too important to me."

"Important to you?" Vee asked. "We're all playing last time I checked."

"Select team coach mean anything to you?"

"Uh, actually, no," Vee answered. "Who is this guy?"

"Aaron Dunkin. He's not only the select coach for our state, but also for the whole Northeast."

"What does that mean?"

Lily sighed. "It means that if I play well, I could get picked for the state tryouts. If I make the state team, I could one day make the Olympic team or play in the World Cup." Lily pointed to the autographed poster of the U.S. National Team hanging over her bed.

"Don't you have to be older?" Vee asked.

"No. If you don't start now, you might never get

noticed," Lily said. "This is a huge opportunity for me, Vee. My dream come true."

"But I thought Chris said he wasn't coming to see anyone in particular."

Lily gave her a look that said otherwise.

"He did? Is the coach coming to see you?"

"Yup." Lily nodded smugly.

"Wow! LJ, that's great! You'll make it for sure." Lily smiled and laid out her socks, shin guards, shorts and cleats. She even went into her secret stash of brand-new ponytail holders. She beamed with satisfaction when she was finished. Everything was just perfect.

Then out of nowhere her bedroom door opened with a crash as Billy charged in, making Lily jump like a monkey.

"Check this out!" he yelled, waving something in his hands.

"Get out of here!" Lily screamed at her brother.

"Vee, check this out!" He recognized an ally.

"What is that?" Vee asked, jumping off the bed.

"It's so cool, you will not believe it. It's so cool

my hands are frozen." Billy danced around the room waving his arms, and Lily laughed in spite of herself. Vee cheerfully took the bait.

"Let's see it." She held out her hand to Billy. He handed her a battered old book.

"Wow, Bill," Vee teased. "That is some cool stuff. I think I see some actual ice in here."

"I know!" Billy answered, oblivious. "Dina found it in the trunk of her car and gave it to me!"

"What is it?" Lily asked.

"Stuff she gave me and not you."

Lily grabbed the book. "Let me see that." She flipped it over in her hands and read the title. *"Inspirational Sayings for a Fulfilling Life.* Oh yeah, quite a score," she said sarcastically, tossing the tattered paperback on the bed.

"Want to hear one?" Billy asked, jumping up next to Vee.

"No!" Lily said.

"Yeah!" Vee yelled at the same time.

"It's alphabetical," Billy announced, making sure to sound out every syllable: *al-pha-be-ti-cal.*

Vee scrambled next to Billy. "Let's try *v* for *victory*!"

"Here's one," he said. Vee and Billy read together. Lily watched as they put their two heads close, the blue-black of her friend's hair bringing out Billy's Irish red. Lily was annoyed. Why did her brother have to come barging into her room like that? The one place in the house she could call her own. And why was Vee reading his dumb book? Who cared about a bunch of silly sayings?

"Isn't this one from one of those commercials with the lizard?" Vee asked, pointing to a page. Lily sighed.

"You guys are too deep for me," she said, leaving Vee and Billy and heading downstairs. Dina was reading in the living room. Lily's mom was still on her butterfly hunt in California.

"Hey, Dina."

"Hey, squirt. Your mom called," her aunt said, carefully folding up the map she'd been looking at.

"Why didn't you get me?" Lily asked.

"Sorry. She couldn't talk for long. Said she's hot

on the case of the smuggler but will be on the red-eye Sunday."

"Red-eye?"

"The overnight flight home," Dina explained. "You get so exhausted trying to sleep like a sardine in a tin can your eyes are red when you land."

Lily flopped down on the couch with the subtlety of a wrecking ball.

"Rainy day blues?" Dina asked.

"I'm just anxious for tomorrow's game. The select coach is coming just to see me."

Dina raised her eyebrows. "Just to see you? That's a pretty big deal."

"I can't wait until kickoff," Lily told her.

"Who are you playing?" Dina asked.

Dina waited for a response, but Lily didn't answer. She was lost in thought, picturing herself scoring goal after goal.

chapter 8

"It's not fair!" Lily complained to her coach. "Why today?"

Beth was stuck at a family reunion and wouldn't make the game until halftime. Lily would start in goal against Castle Creek. She felt set up. Chris must have known: that's why he had been having her practice in goal.

"LJ, like I've said before, you're the best athlete we have. I need someone who can keep us in this game until Beth shows up. But the team needs you. Teamwork, remember?"

Lily slouched on the bench as Chris handed her the red jersey with the long sleeves and padded elbows. Her eyes scanned the crowd for the select coach. Legend had it he wore only white. She jumped when she felt Chris put a hand on her shoulder. "Cut down the angle and get your body behind the ball. Just like defending. Only this time you can use your hands. You'll be great, LJ. I know it."

Lily took a deep breath and tiptoed onto the field, trying her best to avoid the white lines. The rain had finally stopped, but the field was muddy and slick. Her feet felt heavy, and all her normal pre-game anticipation morphed into a serious pout. She put on the gloves and took her place in front of the goal. Vee waved to her from half field, and she halfheartedly raised her hand to respond. The referee took that as the sign she was ready and blew the whistle.

Game on.

On instinct, her legs woke up as soon as the girls started moving. She was tempted to follow the ball but had to settle for watching from afar. Lily had to admit the view was different from the end of the field. She could take in the whole scene: she noticed the bevy of too-tan Brookville moms dotting the sidelines, video cameras armed and ready. Skinny, manicured and electronically loaded seemed to be the theme of the town ladies. Lily mentally lumped the dads at the game in two categories: Berries and Nuts. The Berries were the ones with BlackBerries in holsters attached to their hips who whipped them out like gunslingers in the Old West. Tabitha's dad was a Berry. He watched the game in two-second intervals, bobbing his head up and down as he furiously typed out an e-mail. She noticed that the Berries like Mr. Gordon tended to remain standing to better camouflage their feigned interest in anything other than Wall Street woes and wages.

The Nuts were the dads who took the game way too seriously. They wore dark tracksuits and squatted along the sidelines so that their heads stuck out like the center of a chocolate doughnut. They screamed like lunatics. Even Lily could peg these dads as the ones who never got to play much as kids. They took it all way too seriously. But at least they were *there*. Of course, Lily's parents were nowhere to be seen. Looking around, she spotted her own motley cheering crew of Dina, Pop Pop and Billy. Lily released a heavy sigh as she saw Billy sneaking off behind the bleachers.

Lily tried to concentrate on the field. She could see the layout of all the positions, who was running and who was goofing off. She could also see that Castle Creek had some great players—in particular a halfback with short brown hair who seemed to be in the middle of every play. Lily remembered that was Molly Barrelton and admired the way she worked to get open.

Next to the team benches, she finally found the man in white. He had pale skin and thick dark hair with a pencil behind his ear. He stood alone with his clipboard and after every big play would carefully take the pencil from behind his ear, mark something down and put the pencil back. State Select Team coach. No doubt.

She noticed her own coach was more agitated than normal, pacing the sides and yelling in his panic voice. It took her a minute to notice that he was bellowing at her.

"Wake up, LJ!"

In her reverie, Lily had become so engrossed by analyzing the sideline scene she had inched farther and farther from the goal. She'd stopped watching the game at the precise moment Molly Barrelton got loose on a breakaway: she had the ball at half field and was heading straight for goal. Lily peeked over her shoulder and realized she was completely out of position. Backpedaling as quickly as she could, she tripped, landing with a thud on her backside. She heard a collective gasp from the sideline.

One voice, however, was loud and clear.

"LJ, get up!" Chris screamed.

Lily scrambled back to her feet as Barrelton closed in. She was thirty yards out now—nearly close enough to shoot. It was all up to Lily. There was no way Sue or the other defenders could catch up with Molly. Lily clapped, hearing the poof as her gloves made contact. She stayed on her toes and moved forward to cut off the angle.

The Moms, Nuts and Berries were all revved up like some kind of giant spectator smoothie. Lily tried to remember Chris's speech from earlier in the week but couldn't think clearly with all the screaming. Something about face lotion?

Molly Barrelton was only about ten yards away now. Lily had to stop this girl. She crouched low, like a cat prepared to pounce in any direction.

Then she remembered what Chris had preached. Keep calm. Keep it together. Maintain equilibrium. Barrelton touched the ball again, and Lily knew this was her chance. If the girl got past her on the next touch, she would score. Lily took a deep breath and blocked out the chaos erupting on the sidelines. The world seemed to slow, and the roars of the crowd dulled to a quiet hum.

The ball floated into the space between the two players and Lily moved forward. Instead of grabbing with her hands, she lunged with her feet. The mud helped Lily slide forward with ease, and Barrelton was taken off guard. Both girls struck at exactly the same instant. There was an awful crunch as they fell to the ground. The wet ball popped free, landing behind Lily and right in front of the goal. There was nothing between the ball and the net but twelve yards of green.

Instinct took over and both girls scrambled to

their feet. It was all about wanting it now. Whoever wanted it more would win this battle. They jockeyed shoulder to shoulder. All Barrelton had to do was get a foot on it. The goal's hungry mouth was open wide.

It was do or die. With a grunt, Lily launched her body through the air—swinging her leg in front of Barrelton and poking the ball to the side. She slid past without any illegal contact, jumped to her feet and then pounced onto the ball.

She stood up and time resumed its frantic pace. She could hear the roar of the crowd. Aunt Dina was making a strange guttural bark, but everyone else was clapping and nodding. Lily noticed with satisfaction as the man in white reach behind his ear and took down his pencil. Now there's some equilibrium, Lily thought smugly.

chapter 9

Beth arrived during halftime, and Lily happily handed over the red jersey. The teams were still at a scoreless tie. She readjusted her ponytail as the Bombers took their positions on the field, picking a few pieces of grass out of her hair as she assumed her place next to Vee.

"Uh-oh," Vee said, pointing to a group under a large oak on the far side of the field. "You see that?"

Lily turned and her heart sank. A group of football players were trickling in and starting their warm-up. Griffin Prescott IV's cocky presence was unmistakable as he tossed a football to Mark Gordon.

"Oh, great," she said.

"Don't think about them," Vee said.

"Easier said than done."

"Let's just get a goal and finish this. We can beat these guys."

Both sides took turns attacking without scoring until the Bombers got their chance at the eighty-five-minute mark. Avery and Sue made some magic up the left side and delivered the ball to Vee at the top of the eighteen-yard box. Vee pulled the ball back with her right foot and made some moves Lily had never seen from her before. She dribbled circles around two defenders and connected with a screamer that seemed certain to go in.

The Castle Creek goalie got her fingers on the ball at the last second, though, and tipped it over the bar. Lily saw the select coach take down his pencil and nod approvingly at Vee. Lily knew time was running out. She needed the ball. Now.

Since the goalie had tipped the ball out of bounds and over the goal line, the Bombers were awarded a corner kick. Lily knew the free kick from the corner flag was a great scoring opportunity for her, but only if she put the perfect spin on a banana kick. Yet it was also a perfect chance to use the corner kick as a pass and redirect the ball into the net off a head or foot. She ran over to take the corner kick. Chris waved her off from the far side of the field. "LJ, stay central!"

Lily didn't listen. She trotted over to her teammate Olivia and said, "I got this one."

Olivia looked surprised as Lily snatched the ball from her hands. "But I thought Chris wanted me . . . ?" she questioned.

Chris was yelling from the sidelines now. Again Lily ignored him.

"No worries," she said to her teammate. "I'm going to banana this baby in."

Lily put the ball down in the small corner box and raised her arm to signal she was ready to kick. Her teammates looked unsure but responded by getting into position and lifting an arm to signal they were ready. Lily had dreamed a kick like this a million times. She was going to bend in the shot and win the game.

Lily lifted her own arm to show she was about to kick. She struck the ball. It soared toward the goal and started to drift to the left just as she'd hoped. Lily held her breath. The crowd on the sidelines grew silent. The ball started its long, loopy curve. It was going in!

Lily had raised both arms in victory and let out a cheer when out of nowhere the Castle Creek goalie charged off her line and punched the ball clear.

Suddenly Lily and the rest of the Bombers were caught flat-footed when the ball landed at the edge of the box. The entire Bomber squad had moved into offense. Sitting alone now at midfield was Molly Barrelton. A smile flashed across her face as a Castle Creek defender sent a long leading pass down the line. Molly took off like a lioness on the hunt. A sense of sports inevitability filled the air and twisted Lily's gut. Molly would not be denied this time. She dribbled neatly and quickly to the top of the box as Sue and Amelia gave chase.

Beth moved forward from the net, cutting down the angle, watching the attacker's feet. But Molly was quicker. She pulled up and faked a shot that sent Beth leaping to her right. Then, with the ease of an

English professor reciting the alphabet, the Castle Creek star practically walked the ball into the net.

Just like that, the Bombers were losing the most important game of the season.

Chris fumed on the sidelines as Lily got back to midfield. Vee shot her a strange look, but there was no time to talk.

"One minute left, girls," the referee told them, placing the ball down for the restart.

"Pass it to me," Lily said to Vee.

Vee looked to the sidelines, where Chris was trying to rein in his anger and encourage his team.

"I can do it," Lily said.

The whistle blew. It's not too late, Lily thought. Vee delivered the pass and Lily started dribbling. She stepped over the ball to her right and moved left, beating two midfielders.

"I'm open, LJ!" she heard Vee call.

Not today, Lily thought. This one is mine.

Lily moved forward alone, fighting off defenders, practically crashing her way downfield. She did a spin, a pullback, a crossover. She was on fire and getting closer to the goal. The clock was ticking. Only seconds left. She knew all eyes were on her. There was only one more defender to beat now.

"LJ! Pass the ball!" Vee screamed. "I'm wide open!"

She looked up. Vee had tracked Lily downfield and was ten yards off to her left. She was unmarked in the box. Lily's legs itched to pass, but she held back, remembering the select coach had already seen Vee's moves.

Lily put her head back down and forged ahead, going straight at the sweeper—the last defender between her and the goalkeeper. All she had to do was beat her and take the shot. Moving quickly, she kept the ball close to her feet and then changed her pace, trying to draw the girl forward. Lily blocked everything out—the scene became like a photo, and the image of her scoring loomed large. She would tie the game right now and the select coach would pick her first.

She stepped over the ball with her right foot, pulling the sweeper to her left, then moved the ball forward with her left and closed in to take the shot.

She would save the day. The sweeper was beaten. Or so Lily thought. She moved to get past, but the girl pushed back. Lily's legs slipped in the mud and she started to lose control.

She looked for Vee, but she was covered by two defenders now. There was nowhere to pass.

The ball rolled out of touch.

Lily fought for position but was too late: the sweeper stepped in front and gently tapped the ball back to her goalie, who kicked it wide.

Lily bent to catch her breath and heard two short beeps of the whistle and then one long one. The game was over. The Bombers had lost. Lily looked to Vee, who shook her head and walked off the field. Chris kept his back to the field as he cleaned up the cones and balls by the bench. Her aunt Dina was strangely silent, but Lily noticed old Pop Pop eyeing her over his shoulder. She saw the football players turn back to their warm-up with a collective shrug.

Lily searched for one last person. It was easy to spot the man in white standing off on his own. The coach stood unmoving for a moment as if deep in thought. She wondered what he was thinking. Perhaps he saw how great all her moves were? Lily stopped. The coach stared at her for a long moment and then slowly and unmistakably steadied his clipboard, flipped his pencil and started to erase.

chapter 10

Lily counted the cracks in the ceiling and wondered how long she could stay buried under the blanket. It was Monday morning, and she was sure she couldn't face school or, worse, soccer practice later that afternoon.

Her coach hadn't spoken much after Saturday's game, but his long skinny face had flashed opinions like a Times Square billboard, every gesture broadcasting his disappointment. The only one who even talked to her was Tabitha Gordon, who really dug some of Lily's moves that last minute of play. To say she missed the point was the understatement of the season.

Lily still had a hard time reliving the weekend. It all felt a little surreal—like she was an avatar in some other twelve-year-old's imaginary life. First she blew the game and handed the Bombers their first loss of the season. Then she had to watch as the select team coach asked to speak only with Vee Merino and Molly Barrelton after the game. Finally, the coup de grace of the weekend de crap came during Sunday dinner in the form of a bombshell from Aunt Dina.

"Everyone, I've got some exciting news," she'd said casually. Lily was poised to dig into her dad's latest effort—pesto lasagna with sausage—but held her fork and looked around the table. When her dad took an unusually large gulp of wine and Pop Pop didn't flinch, Lily got the distinct impression that this "exciting news" was only "news" to Lily and her brother. Their mom was still in Los Angeles.

"What is it, Aunt Dina?" Billy had asked, taking the bait.

"Well, I've been presented with an exciting opportunity to be the head environmental engineer on the new Hudson River Rail Tunnel."

"Wow! That's great!" Billy said, but then looked confused. "Uh, what does that mean?"

Dina laughed and explained that she would be

investigating the long-term impact the proposed new rail tunnel connecting New Jersey and Manhattan would have on the shoreline. She was going to be moving to an apartment in Hoboken during the week. She could come back to the suburbs on weekends. It was only going to be for a few months, but she was thrilled at the chance to head up the team on such an important project. Billy's face still registered bewilderment.

"It the opportunity of a lifetime," Dina said. "I can't pass it up."

"Opportunity!" Billy shouted, knocked over a glass and leapt from the table. "Be right back!" he said, vaulting up the stairs.

Lily could see Dina was proud of her new assignment and was happy for her aunt until she noticed several battered suitcases in the foyer. Wheels started turning and alarm bells ringing.

"Wow, Pop Pop," she said hopefully, "are you excited to be going with Dina?"

There was an ominous silence at the table. Lily looked at her grandfather. She knew he was selectively hard of hearing. Plus, he was eating. She tried again.

"POP POP, ARE YOU EXCITED TO GO TO HOBOKEN WITH DINA?"

His focus was laser sharp. His head never moved. That lasagna was toast. Lily stole another glance at the suitcases. Dina mopped up Billy's spilled water. Her father took another large sip of wine.

"Well, kids," he said, "I wish your mother was here, but . . ."

Lily stared hard at her father. He wouldn't.

"Wait, where's Bill?" her father asked, looking around. On cue Billy burst back into the room.

"Pop Pop is going to move in with us for a while," he announced finally.

"Great!" Billy shouted, waving his quote book in the air. "I saw it in the *O*s."

"Yeah, great," Lily said to herself in a tone even the truly deaf couldn't miss. She put her fork down and did a little family math. They lived in a small three-bedroom house.

"Where . . ." Lily had started to ask when Pop Pop came to life.

"Est!" he yelled, pointing to his empty plate.

"You want more pasta, Pop?" her dad asked, trying to decipher the old man's excitement.

"Est est est!" Pop Pop yelled again.

Liam looked at Dina. Dina squinted at Pop Pop. Lily wanted to scream.

"Dad." She tried to get his attention.

"Eccoci qua!!" her grandfather shouted, moving his hands excitedly—gesturing was an integral part of his personal language.

Dina smiled and nodded. "Yeah, I think you're right. Pop thinks this is the best dish you've ever made."

Pop Pop nodded and put down his napkin. He made a motion with his fingers and then winked at Lily. Dina translated, "But he said to take it easy on the garlic."

"You know," Liam jumped in quickly, "I was thinking the same thing. I was watching the news as I cooked and sort of got carried away by—"

"Dad?" Lily tried to interrupt.

"Found it!" Billy yelled.

"Found what?" Dina and Liam asked in unison.

"The quote!"

"What quote?"

"About opportunity! Right here after all the ones about old age."

"Oh, great, let's hear it," Dina said, and even Pop Pop seemed interested.

"Dad!" Lily could feel the rash of heat traveling from her shoulders up her neck.

"The only sure way to miss success is to miss the opportunity," Billy read.

"Amen to that," Dina said, and raised her glass.

"DAD!!" Lily couldn't take any more.

"What?" her father said, startled. "Why are you shouting, LJ? I've warned you about that temper."

Lily took a deep breath and tried to calm down. "Where exactly is Pop Pop going to be staying?"

"In your room."

Lily's head started to spin.

"But Dad!" she started to argue.

He just held up his hand like a crossing guard. "It's temporary."

"Where exactly am I supposed to sleep?"

"With Billy. You can use the top bunk."

"Why can't he stay in Billy's room?" Lily asked, glancing away after catching the old man picking sausage out of his dentures.

"Because old men need to go a lot at night. Your room has a bathroom."

Lily wished she hadn't asked. She felt like her world was crumbling into her plate of half-eaten lasagna.

"But Daddy." Lily whined a feeble protest. She lowered her voice and held her hand to the side of her face. "Pop Pop stinks."

Her father put his hand back in the don't-walk position.

"Enough. This is what's happening, LJ, and your mother I and expect you to cooperate."

"When?" Lily asked, already knowing the answer was that very night.

The next morning, Lily lay on her little brother's top bunk, images from the game replaying endlessly in her mind. She couldn't shut them off. She'd tried burying her head under the pillow as an escape, but the images just followed. She'd felt so certain she would score and at least tie the game. Why had it all gone so wrong? If Chris hadn't made her play goalie, she would have had a whole other half of offense. It was his fault.

She wanted desperately to talk to Vee but couldn't seem to pick up the phone. She had called while Lily was in the shower on Saturday night, but Lily still hadn't called her back. She was dying to know what the select team coach had talked to her about, but a pang of jealousy hit her like a punch to the stomach. Vee had never said she wanted to be on the state team; she knew that was Lily's dream. Without Lily, Vee wouldn't even be playing for Brookville. Lily felt cheated and angry.

She rolled over and spied a snapshot on her brother's bulletin board. Lily recognized it from the previous summer and a road trip the family had taken to Maine. Her mother was wearing a fuchsia tank top that read Keep Your Proboscis to the Grindstone, and her father was kissing a massive red lobster. Why did her family have to be such a band of freaks? No one else she knew had to share a bedroom with their phrase-spouting little brother, and she couldn't even contemplate the HAZMAT zone that was once her beautiful bedroom.

Lily's mind raced. Maybe if her parents supported her more at the games, she'd have scored. Why can't my parents just have normal jobs like everyone else? she thought. Why do we always have to be so worried about money? Lily was developing a long laundry list of people to blame when she heard the front door slam and a familiar voice call, "Anybody home?"

Mom. Lily had forgotten she was due back this morning.

"Mom!" Lily answered in a yell, bolting up and forgetting she was in the top bunk. She cracked her head on the beam above and let out a sharp yelp. "Ow!"

"Lily!" Her mother flew into the room in a panic. "Oh my goodness, baby, are you okay?"

Lily suddenly broke into tears. She told her mom all about Saturday's loss and not making the select team tryouts. Her mother stroked her face and wiped her tears away.

"Everyone has to lose sometime, honey," her mom said. "You know that. Just be proud of the fact that you and your teammates played your hearts out. You'll get them next time, I'm sure of it."

Lily's tears didn't stop. Her mom kissed her. "What's all this about, sweetie? Did something else happen?"

"Mom, I don't want to share a room with Billy. Why can't Dina take Pop Pop with her to Hoboken? Why does he have to stay here? He smells *old*!"

Her mother's face changed with the speed of Lily's best full volley. She raised an eyebrow and stepped back from the bunk beds. A noise in the hallway startled them both. Pop Pop coughed as he stood in the doorway, a hurt expression on his face. He turned and moved away.

"Lily Antonia James," Lily's mother said ominously. It was never good news to hear her full name at the start of a sentence. "You might want to rethink that last bit."

"Mommy!" Billy burst into the room and hugged his mother. His F.O.M. radar immediately detected a target.

"She in trouble already?" he asked.

Toni James gave her daughter a look that caused her to slink back under the covers.

"Give us a second," her mother commanded, and Billy smiled and skipped out of the room.

Her mother closed the door behind him and came back to the bunks so she and Lily were face-to-face. "Listen, there's a lot more to Pop Pop than you know, and it would do you a lot of good to get to know him better."

Lily's head was pounding like a bass amplifier. She closed her eyes and massaged her temples. Her mom kept going. "Your grandfather has made countless sacrifices for this family that you don't even know about, young lady, and giving up your bedroom for a few months isn't asking much in return. In fact, it doesn't even scratch the surface. We all support one another in this family. We are a team. I thought I taught you that.

Maybe it's my fault for not instilling . . ." Her voice trailed off.

Lily lay still.

"Sweetheart, are you okay?" her mom asked in a worried voice.

"Yeah, Mom, I'm fine," Lily answered, but then recognized her own *O* for *opportunity*.

She struggled to sit up. "Maybe I hit my head a little harder than I thought. But I'll be okay."

"Oh, honey," her mother said. "Don't move. Lie back down. Turn to me."

Lily opened her eyes slowly and felt a pang of guilt when she saw sincere concern on her mother's face. She knew it was a dangerous card to play, but some things just had to be done. She couldn't take any more. She faked a little groan.

"Heavens, are your pupils dilated? Are you going to throw up? Let me go get you some ice! Why do you children always seem to get sick right when I come home?"

Her mother rushed from the room, and Lily knew she was headed to the kitchen supply of prepackaged ice packs.

Lecture terminated. Phew.

Lily was lying on the top bunk savoring the silence when Billy traipsed into the room.

"Nice one," he said, grabbing his quote book from the floor. "You going concussion or flu?"

chapter 11

Lily escaped her mother's grasp after two icings and a bitter Filipino herbal tea that tasted like mothballs. She realized it was time to recover and face her fate and her friends at practice. Her mother seemed happy enough to forget her anger and Lily's injury once she told her mother the tea had done its magic.

"I just knew that tea would come in handy one day," her mom had said with satisfaction.

Lily avoided her teammates at school and made a point of getting to practice just as warm-up was starting. She was hoping to avoid any pre-practice lectures from her coach. She changed into her cleats and grabbed her ball just as Tabitha was walking onto the field.

"You want to warm up?" Lily asked.

"I thought you only warmed up with Vee," Tabitha said, almost shyly.

"Not always," Lily lied. Vee, she knew, was at a dental appointment, but Tabitha didn't need to know that.

"Where does she live again, anyway?" Tabitha asked.

"Oh, in Lakewood somewhere."

"Lakewood?" Tabitha asked, making a face. She passed Lily a looping half volley. Lily trapped it easily and sent back a clean pass low to the ground. Wait until Vee hears I was warming up with Tabitha, Lily thought. She'll see what it feels like to be left out.

Yet her joy was short-lived. Her coach's voice boomed from the bench. "LJ, come here, please."

"Be right back. Gotta go listen to some 'think time' blah blah blah." Lily opened and closed her hands like someone yammering on. Tabitha laughed and picked up the ball to do some juggling.

"Good luck," she told Lily.

"Hey, Coach," Lily said casually as she approached.

"Sit down, LJ."

"But Coach, you always say sitting down makes your muscles cold."

"Sit."

Lily sat on the bench. Chris got up and started pacing in front of her. She couldn't read his face but figured maybe she could try heading off his little speech at the pass.

"I'm sorry about Saturday, Coach. I know I wasn't supposed to take that corner kick, but I just had a feeling it could get it in. It was so close too! I won't miss next time."

"That's right, you won't," Chris responded. "Because you won't be taking it."

He stopped pacing and stood in front of Lily. "You really made a mess last game. And not only because of the corner kick."

"I know," she answered quickly. "I tried to get the ball to Vee, but she wasn't open." That wasn't true exactly, Lily knew, but she wasn't sure what Chris could see from the sidelines.

Chris sighed and sat down next to Lily on the bench. "LJ, you need to stop talking and start listening to me."

Oh, great, here we go, Lily thought. Lecture on the launchpad.

"You're a great player, LJ, a great player. But great players have special problems that ordinary players don't have. Sometimes, in tough situations, players like you are tempted to just take over and do everything themselves. To just try to make a spectacular play all alone to score the goal we need to win the game. Sometimes it works, but usually not. I'll tell you what, though—it's never a good idea."

"Okay, Coach. I hear ya." Lily got up, hoping she could speed this along. Chris put a hand on her shoulder and eased her back down.

"The reason it's a bad idea is because that is not how a team works. We work together as a unit. Each player has her job and her responsibilities. You know that. You play your position and the other girls play theirs, and, if everyone does her job, then the team works like a machine. A machine with a heart."

Lily stared past Chris at her teammates on the

field, laughing, chatting and passing around. Her legs jumped every time one of them thumped the ball. She wished Chris would finish already.

"LJ, when you lose your patience and try to do everything yourself, then the machine doesn't work right. It's broken because the other players don't understand why you've abandoned the plan, why you aren't doing what you are supposed to do. They wonder, should I forget my responsibilities too? Or should I do what I'm supposed to do while Lily gets to take over and hog the ball? They look up to you, and they're confused. And confused players lose concentration and heart and start playing worse."

Lily hung her head. Despite her efforts to block them out, images from the game crept back into her brain. The missed corner. Vee open wide in front of the goal. The confused looks her teammates gave her. She looked down and counted blades of grass. Why was he trying to make her feel worse than she already did?

"I am actually glad we lost that game because if you *had* scored and we had won, you would have thought that you did the right thing. You would have been rewarded for being selfish. It wasn't the right thing to do. It was the wrong thing and we lost, which means I have a chance to teach you something so important it'll help you for your whole soccer career."

Lily moved her eyes to the swoosh on her cleats, but Chris's tone was finally penetrating her sullen brain. She felt worried suddenly. She turned and watched his mouth as the words tumbled out.

"It's easy to listen to me talk and it's hard to maintain your discipline when we are under pressure," he said. "You made bad decisions. Selfish decisions. Your passion got the best of you this time."

Lily had to stop this. "I'm sorry, Coach, I just—"

Chris cut her off. He looked her straight in the eye, holding her gaze. Lily started to get a sick feeling in her stomach. "I know what you wanted to do, LJ. It was obvious. But you weren't doing it for the team; you were doing it for yourself."

"I said I was sorry," Lily said.

"I know you did, but it's not about being sorry. Understand that I am not mad at you."

"You're not?" Lily asked.

"No, I'm not mad at you. You made mistakes— mental mistakes. But I'm the coach, and my job is to help you eliminate your mistakes as much as you can. We only work when we work as a team. You have to learn from this."

"I will, Coach, I promise," Lily said.

"I know you will, LJ, because for the next two games you sit with me."

Lily's eyes flew open. She thought she might throw up. She must have heard him wrong. Her mouth felt dry, and she fumbled for words.

"I . . . I sit with you?" she finally managed to ask.

Chris nodded somberly. "For the next two games you're on the bench next to me."

"But—the championship?" Lily stammered.

Chris took his whistle out of his pocket. He didn't twirl it. He wrapped it tightly around his wrist and gave it a curt blow, announcing the start of practice.

"LJ, I'm suspending you from the team. Pack up your stuff and go home."

chapter 12

Lily grabbed her bag and marched off the field in a whirlpool of fury and humiliation.

Come to the game Saturday in street clothes, Chris had instructed. No uniform. No practicing.

Her teammates had watched in shock as Lily left, and her last image of the field was Chris gathering the girls to inform them of her suspension.

She wouldn't go home. She couldn't face Billy, Pop Pop and their flatulence fantasyland. Instead Lily found herself walking toward Katerina's. That was usually a good sanctuary. Great piles of fall leaves were gathered at the street's edge, waiting to be swept clean. Lily kicked at them with frustration, but they just fluttered away in an unsatisfying wave.

She arrived at the kitchen just as the evening shift started showing up. Aldo, Ramón, José and a few new faces shuffled in quietly and started chopping vegetables, browning meats and gutting fish. They all greeted Lily with *holas* and warm smiles, and if they were surprised to see her standing in her cleats with a dazed look in the middle of the kitchen, they didn't show it.

She went looking for her father. She walked out the back door, down the steps, and found Tomás supervising a produce delivery.

"*Qué pasó, linda?*" he asked.

"*Nada,*" Lily lied.

Tomás gave her a long look. He knew she was supposed to be at practice.

"*Dime, niña.*"

"I was suspended from the team," Lily said quietly.

Tomás nodded knowingly. "This can happen, even to the best," he told her. "Remember Zidane?"

Lily nodded. Her coach had made them all watch it on YouTube: Zinedine Zidane was the legendary French player ejected from the World Cup finals for head-butting an Italian player. It was one of the most egregious and shocking moments in World Cup history. Tomás came over and embraced her. Then he ruffled her hair. "I hope you will use your *cabeza* more wisely."

The back door opened and Lily's father emerged. "I thought you might find your way here," he said. Lily was puzzled.

"Chris called your mom earlier today," he told her.

Oh, great, Lily thought, does everyone already know I got kicked off the team? "It's not fair!" she complained. "I told him I was sorry like a million times."

"I'm sure he thinks it's the best thing for you and for the team," her father said.

"Best for the team?" Lily was incredulous. "I'm the team's best player! There are only two games left, and I'm going to have to sit on the bench for both of them. I'll even miss the championship!"

Aldo stuck his head out the door. *"Un señor está aquí al frente,"* he said.

"I'll go see who's here," Tomás said, leaving Lily alone with her father.

Liam motioned for Lily to sit with him on the

stairs, but she hesitated. The last thing she wanted was another lecture. Surprisingly, her father didn't say a word. He just gathered Lily next to him and hugged her tight.

"What am I supposed to do for the next two weeks?" she asked finally. "I feel so lost."

"Well, you can still play with the guys and hang out with us here if you like," her father said.

Lily tried to smile, but her mouth sagged. "Maybe he'll change his mind. He'll see that the team can't win without me and change his mind. In two weeks we're set to have the big rematch with Castle Creek."

"LJ, I'm not sure you're getting the message here."

"What's that supposed to mean?"

"It means stop feeling sorry for yourself and starting thinking about how you can be a better teammate and a better player."

"How in the world is not playing for two weeks supposed to make me a better player?"

"You're the one who needs to figure that out for yourself."

The door opened and Tomás came out with a long face and a thin envelope. Lily was grateful for the interruption until he looked at her with raised eyebrows and handed the envelope to her father.

"It's from Mr. Prescott," Tomás said. "And he wants to talk to you, not me."

"He's here now?"

"*Sí.*"

Lily's father jumped to his feet, grabbed the envelope and headed back into the kitchen.

The door closed with a bang and Lily hung her head. She could feel Tomás's eyes on her.

"*Ay, niña.*" He sighed. "Why didn't you tell anyone?"

In the envelope was the bill for the broken Heritage sign. It was a whopper. "What in the world were you thinking, LJ?" was her father's first question when he came back outside. The second followed without an answer. "Why didn't you tell me about this when it happened?"

"Because the sign wasn't broken, Dad, it was no big deal."

"No big deal? You think damaging private property is no big deal?"

"Of course I think it's a big deal. But the sign wasn't broken, Dad! I swear. His son was being such a jerk to Vee. I couldn't let him get away with it."

She'd never seen her father so angry. Whatever suspension sympathy he'd had was long gone. "Well, my dear, you are responsible. And you are the one who is going to pay for this."

"Me? How? I don't have any money."

"Come," he commanded.

Lily followed her father into the kitchen. "It's a good thing you have nothing to do for the next two weeks."

"Why?"

"Because you are going to work in the kitchen until you earn enough to pay for a new sign."

Lily sighed. "For how long?"

"As long as it takes."

"But, Dad!"

"No buts. Not only are you suspended, you are grounded until further notice." Her father handed her a scrubbing brush and a pair of gloves. "Get to work."

She opened her mouth to argue but took the look on his face told her to stay quiet. Could this day get any worse?

An hour later, Lily cringed at the waiting pile of gravy-crusted pots and baked-on lasagna pans. She mindlessly grabbed a pot when the pantry door slammed shut.

"Need a hand?" Vee was standing next to her wearing a pair of bright orange gloves and torn sneakers and holding a dishrag.

"You scared me!" Lily said.

"Sorry," Vee said. "My dad told me everything. This totally sucks."

"Tell me about it."

Vee grabbed the nasty lasagna pan and started scrubbing. The two girls washed in awkward silence. Vee tried to break the ice.

"So."

"So what?"

"You never called me back."

"I know, sorry. How was the dentist?"

"Fine."

"Cavities?"

"Nope."

"Gums healthy?"

"I need braces."

"Bummer."

"LJ?"

"We need more soap."

Lily went back to the supply cabinet for an industrial-sized jug.

"LJ?"

"Yeah?"

"Are we going to talk about this?" Vee stopped scrubbing and stared at Lily.

"About what?" Lily asked, dripping sarcasm like thick dishwater grease. "The fact that I'm suspended from the team or the fact that I'm grounded for the foreseeable future? Which of these would you like to talk about first?"

"Let's start with the game," Vee answered.

"No."

"No, what?"

"I don't want to talk about the game," Lily said.

"Why not?"

"We lost. Remember?"

"Yeah, I remember," Vee said. "I was right there, *remember*?"

"What's that supposed to mean?"

"I mean I was there. I was open. Why didn't you pass the ball? I could have tied it and we could have won it in OT!"

"I didn't see you," Lily lied. "Guess you weren't as open as you thought you were."

"I was wide open! I saw you look at me! What's gotten into you?"

"What's gotten into *me*?" Lily fired back. "You were the one showing off for the select coach!"

"So *that's* what this is about?"

Lily was dying inside. She wanted to know every detail of what the select coach had said to Vee, what his voice sounded like, when the tryouts were. The tingle of envy started in her fingertips and flooded her whole body. She started to fume and the stress of the day coiled in the back of her throat like a cobra.

"Maybe I could talk to the select team coach for you? I'll just tell him . . ."

"Tell him what?"

"You know . . ."

"No, I don't know."

"I would just tell him what a great team player you are. Normally," Vee said.

"Normally?"

"Come on, LJ," Vee said, drying off a strainer.

"Listen, Vee," Lily said testily. "Thanks for the hand, but in case you haven't noticed, I don't need any more help from you. You're the reason I'm grounded for the rest of my life washing dishes in this stinky kitchen."

"How is this *my* fault?" Vee asked. "Last time I checked, I never asked you to fire a rocket at that kid's head. Plus, it's not my fault you were a ball hog and I wound up getting picked and you didn't."

The last line stung like a line drive hitting a bare

thigh on a frigid day. "Well, I have better things to do than the stupid select team anyway," Lily said.

"Like hanging out with Tabitha Gordon?"

"Yeah. So what? She's not so bad, actually."

"She's *not so bad*?" Vee asked. "The girl you used to make fun of for doodling on balls and who thinks fish eggs have something to do with *soccer*?"

"You wouldn't understand," Lily answered.

"Try me."

"Just forget it."

"Is that why you didn't call me back?"

"No. Duh. I was busy, that's all," Lily said. "You're not my only friend, you know."

Lily tried to ignore the crushed look on Vee's face and grabbed a dishrag.

"What's that supposed to mean?" Vee asked.

"I guess you just don't get it, Vee," Lily said. She looked at Vee up and down, then turned away. "It's a Brookville thing."

Vee stood still as shocked tears filled her eyes. "Oh, dude," she said quietly. Laying down her towel, she slowly turned and left the kitchen.

chapter 13

By the end of her third day as a kitchen worker, Lily's temper was as raw as her fingers. She slammed pots and scowled her way through the tasks, determined to make her father sorry to have her around. Yet Liam James paid little attention to her theatrics, and his only reaction to the constant sighing and moaning was to point at the bill posted on the bulletin board behind his desk.

$399.99.

That's how much she had to earn to pay for the sign. The sign she didn't break. Dishwashing wasn't her only task from hell: mopping the floors, hauling trash and any other torture her father could concoct for a measly five dollars an hour. Her task du jour was washing the restaurant windows, and she struggled to keep the big heavy door open while lugging a giant blue bucket filled with a steaming sudsy concoction.

Lily hadn't seen Vee since their fight, and she was trying hard not to admit to herself how much she missed her best friend. Yet every time she moved to pick up the phone, she got a pit in her stomach and reminded herself Vee was the reason she was in this mess in the first place.

Lily was also trying hard not to think about soccer, but that was like a fish pretending it didn't miss water. The lecture from Chris replayed in her mind like a CD on repeat.

Suspended. Suspended. Suspended.

On the bench.

On the sidelines.

Off the team.

A small soapy tidal wave lurched to the ground and soaked Lily's sneakers. "Oh, great," she muttered to herself. She shook her foot to get rid of the water and casually looked down the street to make sure the coast was clear.

To the right, the mailman. No problem.

To the left, *nada*.

Lily pulled her cap down low and her jacket collar up high and quickly turned her back to the street. She lifted the squeegee and got to work, praying no one she knew would walk by. This is beyond humiliating, she thought, grateful to know, at least, that all her teammates were in the middle of the grueling midweek practice.

She soaped the window in a giant arc that reminded her of the center circle of the field. With the first stroke of the squeegee, Lily told herself she was glad to be missing the sprints and drills and speeches. In the next swipe, she longed for a good game of two-touch. She missed the feel of her cleats on the grass; she missed the sound that ball made when she hit it right on the laces. Lily had lost herself sulking in the suds when there was a loud tap on the window. She tumbled backward with a start. Her father was on the other side pointing upward. "Make sure you go all the way to the top of the window."

Lily looked up and shook her head. "I can't reach."

"Then come inside and get the ladder."

Lily got the distinct impression her father was enjoying this torture. She put the squeegee in the bucket and slowly walked inside. Her dad was rummaging through a closet. She considered closing the door and locking him inside.

"Here," he said, holding out a stepladder. "This should do it."

Lily just stood with her hands by her sides.

"Take it," her father commanded.

Lily didn't budge. "Dad, I really think this has got to be against the law or something."

"Get back to work."

"Ever heard of child labor laws?"

"Ever heard of corporal punishment? Perfectly legal," her dad shot back.

"This is so totally and completely unfair!" Lily whined.

"Life's not fair. Get used to it. And don't leave any streaks."

Lily dragged the small metal ladder outside, forgetting this time to make sure the coast was clear.

"Hey, LJ!" said a chipper voice.

Lily nearly fell to the sidewalk. Standing outside Katerina's was Tabitha Gordon. Her mom's giant black car was parked across the street, and Rini gave her a bright wave from the driver's seat. Embarrassment flew through Lily's body, landing with a red flush on her cheeks.

"What are you doing here? Did practice get out early?" she asked Tabitha, looking around.

"Oh, I have a ballet recital this afternoon. I'd skip it, but my dad is taking off work to be there."

"Wow, that's nice of him."

"Well, not exactly. He's only going to make sure I show up. So annoying."

"Yeah, well . . ." Lily stammered, holding up a squeegee.

"I know," Tabitha said with sympathy. "You have to work to pay off that sign."

"I didn't break it."

"I know."

Lily just nodded. Her preference would have been to curl up and die on the pavement. She couldn't believe Tabitha Gordon, of all people, was witnessing her washing windows in the middle of Brookville. Tabitha had probably never washed a dish in her life, much less a window, Lily thought.

"So, we missed you at the last practice," Tabitha said, oblivious to Lily's dismay. "Did like a million sprints."

"Listen, Tabitha, I'd love to chat, but Attila the Dad is on my case today," Lily said, gesturing inside. Hearing about practice gave her a bellyache.

"Yeah, okay," Tabitha answered. "So it really sucks about the suspension. Totally unfair. But I was thinking . . ."

"What?"

"You might have some time to help me over the next two weeks? . . ."

"Help you with what?"

"Remember when I wanted to ask you something at my house?"

"Sure. You asked me to go see your game room."

"Well . . ."

"That wasn't really it?" Lily finished the sentence for her.

Tabitha nodded and had begun to speak when there was another loud tap on the window. "You missed a spot," Attila mouthed.

"Okaaay," Lily said in surly reply.

"Dads," Tabitha said in sympathy.

"No kidding."

"So anyway . . . it looks like I might get some real playing time this week," Tabitha said, looking to Lily like she was trying to build up her courage.

"And?"

"I was wondering if . . . you would . . ." Tabitha looked down and hesitated. "Since we're teammates and all . . ."

As she bowed her head, Lily gasped. Tabitha had unblocked the view of a black dirt bike weaving down the sidewalk.

"Oh, perfect," she muttered.

"What?" Tabitha whipped her head around. Griffin Prescott IV skidded to a halt and sized up Lily, her bucket and the squeegee.

"Well, well," he said. "If it isn't Brookville's newest washerwoman."

"You know I didn't break that stupid sign."

"*No es mi problemo,*" G-4 said with a bad accent and snide laugh. He did a jump off the sidewalk. "See ya."

"Man, that guy makes me mad," Lily said, feeling suddenly hot in the fall air.

She raised the squeegee over her head. All the simmering frustration from the week headed for a boil. He was still close enough to hit. What difference would it make, anyway? She couldn't play soccer, she was stuck in this kitchen . . . why shouldn't she make him pay? She held her arm aloft and revenge flashed before her eyes. As she moved her arm forward, a hand grabbed her wrist and held it back.

Lily looked to find Tabitha behind her. "I'm pretty sure you don't want to do that," she said.

Another really loud bang on the window.

Her father had witnessed the whole exchange and was eyeing her with a military-school-is-in-your-future glare. Lily lowered her arm and was stunned to catch her own reflection. She hardly recognized the contorted face and the ugly stance. She was trying to place the squeegee back in the narrow bucket when the door to Katerina's flew open with a clatter.

"Get inside this instant," her father commanded.

"But, Dad . . ." Lily tried to protest. "I just need a second to talk to—"

"Now!" her father barked. Lily knew this was no time to argue. She turned to Tabitha, but her friend was already walking away.

"Tabitha!" Lily called after her. "Wait!"

But the door to the big black sedan closed and the car slowly pulled away.

chapter 14

Saturday morning was one of the most beautiful days Lily could remember. The sun was high and the wind was low. A perfect fall day and a perfect day for soccer. For everyone except Lily. She'd never dreaded a game in her life.

Until now.

The Bombers were facing the Lockwood Tigers—a good matchup that usually ended with a win for Brookville. A win or a tie would send Brookville to the championship and a rematch against Castle Creek. A loss and they would play for third.

Lily wore a dark blue sweat suit so at least she'd look like part of the team. She slid onto the bench next to Chris right before kickoff. Her coach acknowledged her with just a curt nod, then got up and called out the lineup. Vee was up front, with Amelia as the other striker in Lily's place. Sue was out with an ankle sprain, so Olivia was taking her place in the defense. Tabitha would play right wing, the outside striker position. Lily couldn't ever remember Tabitha starting in a game. She usually came in toward the end, when she couldn't do too much damage. She must be so excited, Lily thought. She watched as Tabitha straightened out her shin guards, stealing nervous glances toward the sidelines. Lily followed her eyes and spied the regular granola mix of Nuts and Berries dotting the sidelines. In the back of the pack was Mr. Gordon. He was standing on the soccer sidelines but watching his son's football practice on the other field.

The teams took to the pitch, and things got off to a sloppy start. The girls were crowding around the ball like six-year-olds. Neither team could string two passes together, and it seemed like the ball spent more time out of bounds than in play. Lily felt a tinge of satisfaction. The Bombers were a mess without her.

The Tigers, with the requisite orange and black uniforms, were the first to get their act together and spent most of the first half on the Bombers' end of the field. Lily watched Vee trying to get some offense going. Her buddy was working hard. It seemed like she never stopped trying to get open. She never stopped cheering her teammates on, no matter how severely they were under attack.

Tabitha, on the other hand, just looked lost and terrified. Every time the ball came close to her, she would run down the line away from the action. It was as if she was afraid of the game. Lily willed her to get in there, but the Tigers defender invariably stepped up and sent the ball back into the Bombers' box.

"Oh, come on," she heard a voice call. "If you're going to play, then get in there!"

It was Tabitha's father, in between e-mails. Tabitha's head snapped up and she looked to Lily like she wanted to shrink down into her uniform and hide. Chris was instantly on his feet.

"Way to stick with it, Tabitha," he called. "You're doing great, but you're running away from the action. Check back to the ball and you'll be off to the races."

Lily saw Tabitha nod and stand a little taller. The Tigers lost the ball out of bounds—Bomber throw-in. Tabitha raced to the sidelines to take it. She lifted the ball over her head with both arms and then launched it forward. Immediately, the whistle sounded.

"Illegal throw. Have to keep both feet on the ground. Orange ball," the referee announced, pointing to Tabitha's feet.

Tabitha looked to the sidelines. Her father was holding both hands over his eyes, as though he couldn't bear to watch anymore. Then, with a shake of his head, he turned his back in order to watch Mark Gordon's football practice on the adjacent field.

Once the ball was back in play, Chris sat back down on the bench next to Lily.

"She knows never to lift her feet on a throw-in. He's totally psyching her out," Chris muttered. "She'd be better off if he didn't show up." Lily thought of her own parents. She'd give anything to have them come see her play.

Suddenly Chris was on his feet, rushing onto the field.

Player down.

Vee.

Her coach rushed to Vee's side. It looked like she was holding her ankle. Lily held her breath. Not Vee. Lily strained to see as Chris helped her to her feet. Vee walked gingerly for a few paces and then nodded that she was okay to play.

"That trip was intentional!" Chris yelled to the referee. "You need to get control of this game."

"That's enough, Coach," the referee replied. "Drop ball."

The ref had decided no one was at fault, so both teams prepared for him to drop the ball between two opposing players. The girl with the quickest feet would win the battle and control the ball. Avery stepped forward to take it for the Bombers, and Lily felt a pang. She was the best drop ball winner on the team.

Avery won the face-off, though, and the Bombers finally worked the ball into the Tigers' half of the field. Chris came back to the bench.

"The ref is losing control of this game. That number six is all over Vee. She totally brought her down from behind. Could have broken her ankle or wrecked her knee," her coach said. She could hear the emotion in his voice but noticed his tone stayed steady.

Neither team was able to score by the time the halftime whistle blew.

The Bombers came over for water and gathered around their coach. Lily was relieved to see Vee walking without any limp. She watched the eyes of her teammates as they listened to Chris.

"Listen, I know this isn't our normal lineup," he said. "But we can take this team if we just play our game. The first half is over. We got the jitters out and we're still even on the scoreboard. Let's just go back out there and work together. Tabitha, remember to stick with the outside defender if she sneaks forward. Vee, keep looking to the outsides. Olivia, keep switching field, don't just go up the middle. All of you remember, you girls are a team. Look to each other and move as one. You can win this game if you do that."

The Bombers huddled together, and Lily stood silently to the side as they refueled on orange slices and Gatorade. It was a strange sensation watching her team as an outsider. The whistle blew and the girls took to the field. Lily noticed Tabitha still looked uneasy.

"Does she always look like that?" Lily asked Chris.

"When her father is watching, she does."

"How do you know?"

Chris looked at Lily and smiled for the first time. He bent his long neck to her. "Because I watch everything and everyone, LJ."

"You do?"

"Of course I do," Chris said with a grin. "I'm your coach."

The second half looked like a different game. The Bombers were more aggressive. Vee was in the middle of every play. She was making passes up and down the field. Reese made an overlapping run down the left-hand line. "I'm open, Vee!" she called.

Vee sent a long pass without even looking up.

Reese picked it up and fought her way to a Bombers corner kick. Olivia looked to the sidelines, and Chris nodded. Olivia would take the kick. The team fell into position, just like they'd done in practice a hundred times. Lily saw then how she'd caused so much confusion when she took the kick against her coach's wishes.

Olivia put in a cross, and Vee was able to control it at the top of the box. Instead of taking the shot, she faked it and made a beautiful pass to Amelia. Amelia hit the ball without even taking a dribble, and the Tigers' goalie barely got a finger on the ball, tipping it over the goalpost at the last possible second. The Bombers were getting closer, and they could feel it. Even Tabitha was in the middle of the action. She wasn't half bad, Lily noticed, when she stuck out those long ballerina legs.

Chris sat next to Lily again. "Beautiful pass, Vee. Man, she makes everyone look good."

Lily watched Vee. He was right. She was completely unselfish. Darting around the field, she was constantly making things happen. Lily had been taking Vee's hard work and energy for granted, she realized.

The Bombers kept pounding, and Lily felt herself getting swept up into the action. She wasn't watching as a player now; she was screaming like a crazed fan.

Just as it seemed that a Brookville goal and win was inevitable, the Tigers' right halfback stole a pass and made an arching run down the line. The crowd jumped to their feet.

"Tabitha! That's your mark!" Chris called.

"Stop her!" Lily yelled.

Tabitha gave chase. The girl in orange and black got the ball at midfield and took it straight down to the corner. Tabitha closed in but was too late. By then, the Bombers' sweeper had no choice but to leave her position in the middle of the field and face the Tiger. There was now a gaping hole in the center of the field. The girl saw the opening and quickly passed the ball sweetly back to her center mid. The girl touched it once and shot. A rocket to the upper-right-hand corner. Beth never had a chance.

Tigers 1, Bombers 0.

Just like that, Brookville went from destined to score to losing by a goal in the final minutes of the game. The entire field energy shifted. The Tigers were regenerated. The Bombers deflated. Lily knew just how they felt.

Chris tried to rally the troops. "Heads up, girls! We have lots of time! Vee, let's get one!"

Vee sprinted back to midfield with the ball, but the referee had to wait until all the Bombers were back on their side of the field. Lily felt Tabitha's pain as she walked slowly back to midfield. Her paces looked heavy, and defeat circled her shoulders.

"That's all right, Tabitha," Chris called. "Get back in the game now."

Tabitha lifted her head slightly. She gave Lily a weak smile, but her eyes darted to the sidelines. Mr. Gordon was leaving the game in the direction of the adjacent field where her brother Mark's football team was now running wind sprints. He'd clearly had enough of his daughter's soccer exploits.

The referee blew the whistle, and Tabitha started

toward the bench. She must have assumed she was being subbed, Lily thought.

"No. Tabitha, stay in," Chris commanded. "We'll get 'em."

Again, Lily was amazed at how much coaching didn't have anything to do with actual soccer. Tabitha slowly took her position, and the referee restarted the game.

It was do or die now for the Bombers. They had to score to make it to the league championship. A tie would be enough, but a loss wouldn't cut it. The Tigers were invigorated and playing with confidence, but the Bombers were the better team. Even without Lily. Vee kept working and with only a couple of minutes left in the game sent a neat cross to Amelia, who had taken over Lily's position. Amelia was in perfect position and nailed a sweet shot right past the outstretched Tigers keeper.

Goal!

The final whistle blew soon after, signaling the end of a tied match; no overtime for regular season games. But the tie was enough to send the Brookville

Bombers to the championship game. Lily was exhausted. She felt as tired as if she'd played every minute. Eleven spent and sweaty girls exited the field. They'd nearly lost the chance to make the finals but pulled it off in the eleventh hour. Tabitha's head still hung low as she walked off the field. Lily noticed that Vee gave her a friendly pat on the back. Vee makes everyone else look good, Chris had said.

Do I? Lily wondered.

chapter 15

"*Don't move, please,*" Lily's mom whispered as she dabbed with the needle. "I'm so close, and the slightest air current will send the wing flying. Again."

It was Tuesday afternoon. Lily watched with fascination as Toni James applied a minuscule drop of glue to the butterfly thorax while flattening the bright blue wing with a toothpick.

"This is a blue morpho," her mother whispered. "From Panama. It came to me with a detached wing. But I think I can fix it."

Lily leaned forward to look at the specimen. The blue wings were nearly the size of an outstretched hand.

"It's huge," Lily said.

Her mother nodded as she applied another dab

of glue. "It's not the biggest morpho, but it is beautiful. This one is *M. cypris*. And I have to set it perfectly flat or else the color will be wrong. It's iridescent," she said with a twinkle.

Finally, her mom leaned back and exhaled. "Okay, come on in."

Lily hesitated. "You sure?"

"Really. It's safe now," she said, gesturing to her daughter to join her at the table.

Lily wrinkled her nose. Her mom laughed. "Oh, that's the glue. But you know me—I only use a water-soluble, biodegradable, repulpable, water-bearing colloidal hydrogel material."

Lily opened her eyes wide.

"You definitely don't want to eat it. It's not the best glue—which is why it's taking me all day—but it's safe to use in the house with my babies around."

Lily made another face.

"You don't like that? Well, sorry. You'll always be my babies, no matter how old you get." Her mother held up the specimen. "So, what do you think?"

"Pretty. But a little crooked," Lily replied.

Her mother looked down and glared. "You're right. Have to start over. Again. But I have time. It's a model for a school presentation I'm doing next week in Tulsa."

"When do you leave?"

"Sunday night. So don't worry, I'll be here for the big game."

Lily shrugged. "I'm not even playing."

"It's your team, isn't it?"

She nodded.

"Then we'll find a way to be there. At least for moral support," her mother said, examining the blue morpho.

"Did it really take you all day to set one butterfly?" Lily asked, changing the subject.

"Yep. And as you pointed out, it's crooked."

"It looks okay," Lily said, feeling bad.

"Okay? Well, I don't know about you, but just 'okay' is not good enough for me," her mom said, peering over her glasses. "You can understand that, can't you, Lily?"

Lily shrugged. "Yeah."

"So Dad called to say he'd never seen better or faster dish washing and potato peeling in his life. Maybe you'll be a chef like him one day."

"Are you kidding?" Lily asked, shocked. "No way. He's making me go back to wash the prep dishes. It's endless. I can't wait to get out of there and . . ."

"Back on the field?"

Lily smiled. She wanted to play so badly her feet hurt.

"Mom, I really think I've definitely learned a lot since I've been suspended. I've spent a lot of time thinking over the last two weeks."

"About what?"

"About growing up. I'm ready."

Lily's mom smirked a little but tried to hide it. "Today?"

"Yes," Lily said seriously. "I really am. I'm ready."

"Well, that's terrific, honey," her mom said, laying out a new set of toothpicks and remixing the glue paste with water. "Help me get this set up."

Lily held the frame steady and watched her

mother realign the beautiful butterfly. "Mom, I was wondering . . . could you maybe call Chris for me?"

Her mom stopped dismantling the display. "You want me to call your coach?"

"Yes. I really really really need to play this weekend. Maybe you can convince him to let me back on the team? You know, tell him I've really . . . matured."

Lily's mom took off her glasses and sat up, stretching her back as she did it. "LJ, your coach is the only one who can decide when you're ready to play again."

"What about Dad? Can't you talk to him and tell him I've washed enough dishes? If you can get him to free me from kitchen patrol, maybe I could jog around the field until Chris changes his mind and lets me play?"

"Is the bill paid off?"

"Almost."

Her mother gave her a hard look.

"Uh, not exactly."

"Then that's between you and your father, sweetie. Growing up means understanding that there are no shortcuts in life. The bill has to be paid. You can't erase your mistakes, LJ. You can make up for them and you can make sure not to repeat them, but you can't just will them to disappear."

"But Mom, I've told you and Dad a zillion times that I'm not the one who broke the sign!"

"LJ, that's not the point, and until you stop saying that, it's clear to me that you are still not getting it. You need to accept that what you did was wrong. Kicking the ball at that boy was wrong. Period. Whether the sign broke or not is irrelevant. It was wrong to lash out in anger. It was really wrong not to tell your father or me what happened. Whether or when the sign actually broke doesn't change those things. So even if I do believe you—which, by the way, I do—it doesn't matter."

"Mom, soccer is everything to me. I can't take any more dish washing. I need to play," Lily complained. "And I miss my teammates."

"So I take it you haven't made up with Vee?"

Lily shook her head no. She wanted to cry.

"Maybe you should call her? Swallowing your pride is definitely an important part of growing up."

Lily shook her head again. She wouldn't know what to say.

"Well, you must have just missed her in the kitchen. Tomás told your dad today that she made the cut. She got picked for the State Select Team."

Lily jerked her head up. "What? Really? How come no one told me?"

"Maybe because no one thought you would be happy. Besides, she just found out. The coach is coming to the game this weekend."

Tears began to well in Lily's eyes. "That was my dream, Mom. Not Vee's. It's not fair."

"I know it was your dream, love. But do you really think you deserved it?" her mom asked. "Maybe it was her dream too. Do you think you deserved it more than Vee?"

Lily thought back to the game and her selfish play. "I guess not."

"LJ, you have all the talent in the world," her mother said. "Anyone with two eyes can see that when you walk on the field, you own the place. Now, I'm not a soccer coach, but I am pretty much the coach of this family. I can tell you all the talent in the world is wasted if you think you can do it all alone. No one can. The world doesn't work like that. Families don't work like that, friendships don't work like that and I'm pretty sure soccer teams don't work like that either."

Lily's mom took another look at the butterfly wing. "Now," she said, "let's straighten this out."

Lily was thinking the exact same thing, only not about butterflies.

chapter 16

Lily searched the library and Starbucks but didn't see any sign of Tabitha until she spotted the sleek black car parked outside the deli.

"Hey, Rini," Lily said.

"Hello, miss," he replied with a big smile. "How is the next Mia Hamm doing today?"

Lily cringed. "I'm fine. But I'm pretty sure Mia Hamm never got suspended."

"That's a good point," Rini said. "But you have a special fire inside. I am sure once you learn to handle it, you will be back better than ever."

Lily nodded. She certainly hoped so. "Um, I'm looking for Tabitha."

"She's at the beauty salon." Rini pointed to the small shop on the corner.

"Oh," Lily replied in a tone that made clear a

beauty salon was pretty much the last place she wanted to be.

Rini laughed. "She will be finished in an hour or so, I am told."

Lily dreaded the idea of approaching Tabitha with all her gossipy school friends. But she really needed to talk to her.

"She's right inside, miss," Rini urged.

Lily scrunched up her face, and Rini seemed to understand her dilemma. "She's at the salon alone today."

Lily glanced inside the beauty parlor window but couldn't see her friend among all the flowers, blowers and tin-covered heads. She steeled herself, took a deep breath and ducked inside as quietly as possible. Bells on the door jangled, announcing her arrival to anyone in a fifty-mile radius.

"May I help you?" a woman asked while looking Lily up and down.

Lily grabbed her ponytail and shook her head no. "I'm just here to talk to my friend Tabitha."

"Ah, yes. Miss Gordon." The woman looked relieved and pointed to the back.

Lily slunk back to the sinks. The whole place gave her the creeps. Lily hated the chemical smells and the prissy women who had certainly never won a drop ball battle in their lives. Lily's mom cut her hair (if you could call battles over half-inch trims haircuts). What was the point of getting your hair done when it was going to get sweaty at practice anyway?

"Hey," Lily said, walking up to the sink.

Tabitha was looking up at the ceiling as a thin pale man massaged her scalp. She glanced out of the corner of her eye. "LJ? What are you doing here?"

"I wanted to talk to you about the game."

Tabitha closed her eyes. "Listen, LJ, I appreciate it, and it's been fun hanging out and all, but I'm pretty sure I'm done with the whole soccer thing."

"What? Why?" Lily asked.

"You know why. I pretty much am the worst player, and let's face it, I'm not exactly used to being at the bottom of any ladder. Soccer was fun, but my future is as a dancer."

Lily could hear defensiveness in Tabitha's voice that worried her. The queen was in court today.

"You can't quit, Tabitha."

"Of course I can. Why not?"

"Because . . ." Lily tried to think of an answer. "We're a team."

"Oh, that's a good one, coming from the girl who got suspended for being selfish."

"I was wrong. I know that now."

"Maybe I just don't like soccer. Not everyone is obsessed like you are, you know?"

"But you do like soccer, Tabitha, I know you do."

The skinny technician gathered Tabitha's hair in a towel and directed her over to a cutting station. Lily followed and watched as he began to comb out the knots.

"Tabitha, I can help you. When I was on the bench the other day, I was watching and I think I know what's wrong."

Tabitha's eyes narrowed. "LJ, I'm trying to relax and get my hair done. I certainly do not want to think about that game anymore."

"I'm sorry . . . I just thought that maybe what you

wanted to ask me the other day was to help you a bit?"

"Well, you're too late. You know what would really help me?" Tabitha asked in an obnoxious tone. "Layers. That's what I really need. Isn't that right, Seth?"

"Absolutely." He laughed. "And an organic deep conditioner."

Lily wouldn't give up. "Remember when we were in your basement and you showed me how to do a pirouette? You just walked up and did it. Without thinking. Without worrying. And it was perfect. You know why? Because you already saw it in your head. You believed."

"Yeah, so?" Tabitha asked. "What does ballet have to do with soccer?"

"It's the same thing. You know what to do on the field. You just don't believe you can do it."

Tabitha's haircutter arrived with the perpetually annoyed look of someone convinced the styling of hair was of vital service to the world.

"What are we doing today, Tabitha?" she sniffed.

"Anything," Tabitha answered.

Lily tried one more time. "I heard your dad at the game. I saw him leave after the Tigers scored."

A sad look crossed Tabitha's pretty face. A silence hung between the girls as the stylist held her scissors aloft, waiting for a cue from Tabitha. Lily looked eagerly at her friend. Tabitha pursed her lips and reached for a tattered tabloid.

"My dad had to talk to my brother's coach. That's why he left the game early," she said. "Look, I just don't feel like playing anymore. Give it a rest. I mean, you really think a girl like me needs tips on confidence from someone like you?"

chapter 17

Lily slowed her pace and stopped halfway between the salon and the restaurant. Standing toe to toe with her reflection, she brushed past freckles and locked onto her own gaze. She pushed in closer. So close, her breath clouded the glass.

Lily didn't believe Tabitha for a second. She wanted to be better at soccer. She actually liked the game, Lily was sure of it.

"Shouldn't you be washing windows?" a voice asked.

Lily spun around to find G-4, Mark Gordon and his buddies straddling their bikes in a semicircle on the sidewalk. With echoes of her mother's voice ringing in her head, Lily moved away, walking quickly and quietly down the street. Katerina's was close by. G-4 got on his bike and jumped the curb, following Lily from the street.

"Late for work? Or is today dish-washing day?"

Lily felt the heat of anger building at the base of her neck. Keep quiet, she warned herself. Lashing out at this jerk is what got you into so much trouble in the first place. The familiar awning was in her sights.

"Not feeling so tough today without your weapon, huh . . ."

She stopped in her tracks and glared at G-4. The smirk on his face was proof enough to her that he was the one who broke the sign. Lily had no doubt at all. She took a deep breath. "I'm sorry I kicked the ball at you. That was wrong."

Her apology threw Griff off. He was silent for a moment, and Lily resumed walking.

"Let's go." Mark Gordon was suddenly beside Griff. "We've got practice."

Lily mentally thanked Tabitha's brother for moving him along, but she didn't say a word. It felt strangely empowering to keep her cool, a new experience, to be sure.

But G-4 shrugged off his friend. "What's the matter?" he said. "Getting kicked off the team has made you soft?"

Lily faced Griff and saw the determination in his eyes. It was then that she knew. He *wanted* her to fight back. He was desperate to show off in front of his friends, and the more she kept her cool, the more foolish he knew he looked.

So she did the one thing she knew would fluster him the most.

She smiled.

Then she turned and walked away.

Lily could hear the boys follow her and was relieved when she arrived at the door to Katerina's. She swung it open and left G-4 behind her.

She headed straight for the kitchen.

"Hi, LJ."

"Is Vee here?" she asked her father.

He looked back and nodded. "She's here, and she's got some great news."

"I know," Lily said. "It's so amazing. And she totally deserves it. You know the best part? Soon everyone in Brookville is going to be talking about the great Vee Merino."

Liam came back and gave Lily a hug. Over her father's shoulder, Lily saw the kitchen door creak open. A petite black-haired girl walked out and locked eyes with Lily. Lily wondered if she'd been listening.

"Dude!" Vee shouted as an electric grin flashed across her face.

chapter 18

Lily's father granted the girls a ten-minute make-up reprieve, so she and Vee went out to the lot behind Katerina's. Vee kept smiling, and the two automatically spread out, taking their favorite spots between the extra parking and the small patch of grass. Lily put the ball on the ground and passed it gently to Vee. It had been too long since it was just two friends kicking around. Vee tapped it back.

"I've been a jerk," Lily said mid-trap.

Vee nodded in agreement. "Did you mean what you said back there?" she asked.

"Of course I did," Lily said. "I'm really proud of you."

"That's funny, because I thought you were mad at me."

"I guess I was just jealous," Lily answered truthfully, passing the ball back. "None of this was your fault. I'm sorry, Vee."

Vee was still smiling, but she looked at the ground now. The ball stopped at her feet. "Well, I've been a little jealous too."

"Of what?"

"Tabitha. I don't have all the stuff she has. I don't have a driver and expensive games or anything like that."

"Believe me," Lily said, "you have no reason to be jealous of Tabitha. If anything, she should be jealous of you. I think maybe she is."

Vee kicked the ball back.

Lily lifted her leg and the ball landed on her sneaker like it was made of Velcro.

"Man, I sure wish you could play this weekend," Vee said. "We're going to need you bad, dude."

"Me too," Lily said. "But Coach has his reasons."

The back door to the restaurant opened and Lily looked up, expecting to hear it from her father. The ten minutes were certainly up. She was surprised to see Tomás instead. "Ladies, there is someone here to see you."

Lily and Vee waited to see who it could be. Tomás opened the kitchen door, and out walked Tabitha Gordon.

"Hey," Tabitha said.

"Wow," Lily whispered, a little unsure.

Tabitha came down the back stairs, hesitating a moment when she reached the garbage cans near the bottom step. Tension hung in the air. Lily held her breath but relaxed as Vee made her move in the unspoken lingo of soccer: she passed Tabitha the ball.

The three girls knocked it around for a while, and Lily was surprised to see that Tabitha was doing really well. Good, in fact. Then Lily and Vee's jaws just about dropped to the floor when Tabitha rolled the ball up her foot and started to juggle. She used both feet and even did a few thigh taps. Plus, she had perfect hair. Vee and Lily were blown away.

"Wow!" Vee cheered. "That was great!"

"Where did you learn to do that?" Lily asked.

"I've been practicing a lot in my basement. With Rini," Tabitha answered with a grin. "My dad thinks I'm doing pliés."

Lily couldn't believe it. "What's your record?"

"Oh, I think like thirty?" Tabitha said.

"Thirty!" Vee and Lily looked at each other, impressed.

"Uh, so why can't you do anything like that during the games?" Vee asked.

Tabitha looked down. "I freak out, I guess. I try to tell my feet and legs what to do, but they just don't seem to listen."

"Well, if you can juggle like that, then you can pretty much do anything," Vee said.

Tabitha shook her head. "No, I can't. I've tried to tell myself I can, but nothing works. LJ, I've wanted to ask you for help for a long time. I just didn't know how to ask. You know, everyone seems to expect . . . certain things from me."

"Like your dad?"

Tabitha nodded. "It was such a big deal for him to let me play this year. Then, in the one game I got real playing time, I totally choked. He's the one pressuring me to quit soccer and focus only on ballet. I wasn't sure at first, but when I saw how amazing you and Vee are, I realized I don't really want to quit."

"Vee got picked for the State Select Team," Lily said.

"That's awesome, Vee."

Lily and Vee's eyes met. "We can help you," Lily said.

"Really?"

Lily and Vee answered together, "Of course!"

Lily thought for a moment, then jogged over to the garbage can goal and counted twelve paces. "Here," she said firmly, and marked the spot with a rock.

"What's she doing?" Tabitha asked Vee. Vee shrugged.

"Soccer is a game of confidence, right? You have to believe you can do it. You have to see it in your head like it's really happening." Lily ran to get the ball and dropped it on the spot.

"Vee, can you play goalie for a second?" Lily asked. "Tabitha, you come over here."

Vee understood right away and jumped into position in the goal, which was really just two garbage cans fifteen feet apart.

"The only thing that's holding you back is this," Lily said, and she pointed to Tabitha's head.

"My haircut? I thought it was pretty happening."

"Yeah, right, very *High School Musical 25*," Lily said. "I meant your brain. It's all in your head."

"Tell that to my feet." Tabitha laughed.

"Remember at the salon when I tried to tell you about doing a pirouette? You can do one with your eyes closed, right?"

"Sure, no problem." Tabitha closed her eyes and executed a perfect twirl. Vee whistled from the goal.

"See? You know you can do it. You can see where you want your arms, your head, your legs. It's all up here. You see it first and then you do it. Easy."

"So if I see myself making great plays, I'll actually make them?"

"Trust me, it's all the same thing. You have to believe it before you can make it happen, and in soccer there's one time where it's true more than any other."

Lily looked at Vee.

"Penalty kicks!" the two friends said together.

"Chris would never let me take a penalty kick," Tabitha said.

"It doesn't matter if you take them or not," Lily replied. "But practicing them will teach you to believe because when it comes to penalty kicks, there's no looking."

"No looking?" Tabitha asked, shocked. "How are you supposed to take a shot without looking?"

"Watch," Lily said. She set up the ball and backed up a few paces. "A penalty kick is just you, the ball and the goalie. As soon as the referee blows the whistle, you get one kick and one kick only, right?"

"Right . . ." Tabitha was confused.

"I know exactly where I'm going to kick the ball. It's my little secret. I see it in my head. It's going in. The goalie, Vee in this case, won't have a chance."

"How do you know?"

"Because I see it happening. I see it right now. I know how I'll approach the ball. I know where it will go. I knew it this morning when I woke up and today at school. I know it now because with a penalty kick, you can never ever look."

Tabitha graduated from confused to bewildered. Lily explained some more. "See that goalie over there?" Vee waved happily. "She's going to watch your every move. She'll watch your eyes. Usually you want to look where you'll shoot, but not now. You can't look. Goalies watch and if you look, you've lost. They'll jump that way, and in a penalty kick, if the goalie knows where you're going, you've already missed. So you have to keep it a secret. A secret only you know. A secret you really believe."

Lily lined up to shoot but kept her eyes on the ball. She never looked at Vee, who was watching her every move. Looking for any clue. Without even lifting her eyes from the ball, Lily stepped forward and fired into the lower-right corner and the inside of the garbage can. It hit so hard the dented lid went flying backward. Goal. Vee never had a chance.

"You see? I didn't look. I didn't have to. I only had to see it in my head. Now you try."

Vee shagged the ball and sent it back. Lily put the ball back on the mark and Tabitha got ready to shoot. Lily watched from the side and made a beep sound for the referee's whistle. Tabitha kept her eyes glued to the ball, took a deep breath and moved to shoot. She stepped forward, head down, face full of concentration. But then she lifted her head at the last second and gave herself away. Vee moved to her right and easily stopped the shot.

Tabitha looked deflated. "See? I can't do it."

"Yes, you can. It takes practice. You didn't learn to do a pirouette in five minutes, did you?"

Tabitha shook her head.

"Well, believe me, I didn't learn to take PKs in five minutes either. Now close your eyes," Lily said.

"Close my eyes? I can't do it with my eyes wide open."

"Trust me. Just close your eyes."

"Okay," Tabitha said, shutting her eyes.

"Now in your mind, line up the ball."

"Okay. Got it."

"Pretend to hear the whistle."

"Beep."

"Take the shot."

"I feel really stupid."

"Do it!" Lily laughed. "You need to see it happening. You need to believe you can do it."

"I can't," Tabitha said.

Lily was getting frustrated.

"Wait!" Vee called suddenly. "I have an idea!" She ran over to Tabitha and whispered in her ear. Tabitha smiled and nodded.

"LJ, you're goalie," Vee said. Lily had no idea what was going on but took her place on the goal line.

"Okay. Here goes nothing," Tabitha said, closing her eyes.

Lily waited for Vee's beep. She waited for Tabitha's eyes to give her shot away, but they didn't. She didn't look up. She didn't keep her eye on the ball either, though. Lily couldn't believe her own eyes when Tabitha took the shot. She'd never seen anything like it before in her life. She'd never imagined anything like it in her life. She certainly never believed *that* could be done. But Tabitha did it all right, and Vee screamed with victory as the ball banged into the garbage can. Lily never had a chance.

Goal.

"How's that for believing, LJ?" Tabitha said with a giant smile.

"Well, if I hadn't seen it, I wouldn't have believed it. That was the first-ever pirouette penalty kick in history!"

chapter 19

Every player, parent and coach knew the deal: winner takes all. No ties allowed. This was the rematch. Defending league champions, Castle Creek was the home team—in white. They were heavily favored to win, having finished a perfect 9–0 season. At 7–1–1, the blue and yellow Brookville Bombers were no slouches, but of course, they would be playing without a key player: Lily James.

The Bombers had banded together and begged their coach to reconsider the suspension, but Chris wouldn't budge. His rule was a two-game suspension, and if that meant Lily missed the final, so be it.

LJ took her place on the bench.

"Let's do it, Bombers!" Lily shouted as the girls warmed up. Lily watched with pride as Vee and Tabitha kicked around. They'd spent hours that week behind the restaurant working on juggling, shooting and anything Vee and Lily could come up with to boost Tabitha's soccer confidence. She must have nailed a hundred penalty kicks.

Lily felt someone's eyes on her. She looked up to see Castle Creek's Molly Barrelton watching her from midfield. She had her short brown hair held back by a white headband. Vee said she'd breezed through the State Select Team tryout like David Beckham in a Tiny Tots camp. Molly put her foot on top of the ball as she watched Lily and gave a nod to the sidelines. Lily didn't have to look long to notice the man in white beaming at Molly.

Lily spied Liam, Tomás, Billy, Dina, Pop Pop and her mother setting up camp on the sidelines. For the first time ever, Katerina's was closing for Saturday lunch so that everyone could attend the game. She couldn't remember the last time both her parents had made it to a game. In fact, she was sure it had never happened before.

The energy on the sidelines was explosive as the teams took the field. Lily had never seen or felt anything like it. The players were jumping up and down in the brisk fall air, warming their bodies and expelling nervous tension. Coaches were shouting before the whistle even blew. Even little kids picked up on the excitement, sticking close instead of running off to play on their own.

One quick beep of the whistle made clear it was going to be one heck of a match. Girls on both sides scrambled for every ball, tackling with no hesitation. Chris had assigned Sue to stick one-on-one with Molly Barrelton, a strategy that seemed to be working. Molly wasn't able to hold on to the ball for long, and Lily thought she looked frustrated. During an early play, Vee dribbled the ball to the corner and sent in a perfect cross. Amelia got her head on it and the ball just glanced off the crossbar.

"Way to go, Vee!" Lily cheered. "Let's go, Bombers!"

The Bomber parents were going bananas. The energy was electric, and Lily was certain her team could score. Suddenly one bellowing voice was heard above the others, reverberating like a church bell in a silent square. "Castle *Creek*! Castle *Creek*!"

Heads on the field turned. A large woman in a bright blue hat sat high atop the bleachers. That woman must be an opera singer or something, Lily thought. The high-pitched voice was like a crowd-silencing aria. All that could be heard was "Castle *Creek*! Castle *Creek*!"

"Play on!" the referee commanded after an instant, and the goalie launched the ball back into play. From there, things started falling apart for the Bombers. Castle Creek began taking cheap shots. Chris was quickly on his feet.

"Ref! That tripping was intentional!" he called after Reese was knocked down at midfield. The Bombers were getting pushed around.

The tide was turning.

The whistle blew. "Player down!"

Lily's head shot up. It was Vee again. The crowd finally quieted as Chris rushed to Vee's side. She was holding her right ankle and a grimace covered her face. Chris helped her to her feet. It was the same ankle she had rolled in the last game.

"I'm okay," she told Chris. Tomás came to the bench with a concerned look on his face. Lily's mom charged over to provide medical backup. "I've got lots of ice!" She reached into her ratty macramé bag.

Vee limped for a few steps and then jogged around.

"She wants to stay in," Chris said to Vee's father as he exited the field. Tomás nodded his okay, and the referee blew the whistle.

Within minutes Castle Creek was on the attack. Molly Barrelton broke free of her mark. Vee was trying to stay in the game but just wasn't herself. The only Bomber playing with any heart was Tabitha. She was running back on defense, pouncing on every ball. Lily looked to the sidelines and saw her mother settle back down. She was not happy to spy Mr. Gordon next to the concession stand. Soon enough Opera Lady started up again, and Lily just prayed for the half to end.

With just two minutes left in the half, the Bombers pulled an offside trap—a move they'd learned specifically for Castle Creek. When the sweeper gave the signal, the defense moved forward to try and trap the Castle Creek offense behind the last defender and draw a penalty. The only problem was Riley's view was blocked, and all the screaming made it impossible to hear Sue yell, "Now!"

Only two girls in the defense moved forward, leaving Riley back by the goal and Molly Barrelton all alone and onside.

A deep booming voice sounded from the other end of the bench.

"Punish that! Punish that mistake!" the Castle Creek coach roared.

Lily cringed.

Castle Creek found the open Molly. Tabitha and Vee gave chase, but they had too much ground to make up. Opera Lady launched into a frantic solo and the Bombers crumbled. Molly breezed past Riley. Beth came off her line, but Molly kept her cool and scored easily.

The whistle blew ending the half, and Castle Creek acted like they'd already won. The Bombers dragged themselves off the field in full bicker. Riley fumed at Sue's call. Olivia glared at Riley. The team was tearing into one another. Even Chris looked dejected. His long face hung down and he shuffled his feet side to side. Lily knew he was trying to think of the right words.

"Girls. I'm going to do us all a big favor and not talk about the first half of this game. I think the best thing we can do is just forget it. We're only down by one goal, and we have the whole second half to win this game. Let's just erase what just happened . . ."

Lily watched the girls' faces. She saw Vee rubbing her ankle. Sue had tears of frustration in her eyes, and Tabitha was staring off to the side. Lily followed her gaze. Mr. Gordon, Mark and Griff had arrived. Oh, perfect, Lily thought. There were only a few minutes left before the second half began. Lily had to do something. These were her girls. She knew Chris wasn't reaching them. They couldn't go back on the field in this state of mind. They'd lose for sure.

There was stony silence after Chris finished his speech. Lily stepped forward.

"Coach, can I say something to the team?" she asked. Chris nodded.

Lily took a deep breath and stared at the ground. She knew she didn't have much time.

"Hey, guys, I'll make this quick. I wish I could be out there with you, but I can't. I made some mistakes and I'm sorry. I apologize to you all for not being on the field. I know I've let the team down. I'd give anything to be playing today. Believe it or not, I've learned more about being a team player by getting kicked off.

"Castle Creek is a good team—and they've got one really loud lady—but that doesn't make them the champions. Not yet, at least. So they scored. So what? This game isn't over by a long shot."

Lily looked at her teammates. Every pair of eyes was on her except one: Tabitha had hers closed. Lily smiled.

"The most beautiful part of this game is that it doesn't just begin or end on the field. We win together or we lose together. We're a team: a team that sticks up for each other, a team that helps each other. A team with heart."

Lily paused and thought for a second.

"So if we're a team with heart . . . hearts beat, right?"

The Bombers all nodded.

Lily put her arm out, palm down. "Well, I say today, we *beat* the tar out of Castle Creek."

Vee stood up and put her hand on Lily's. Tabitha opened her eyes and stood up. One by one, each Bomber joined the pack until it was just a tight circle of players and a pile of dirty hands.

"Everyone close your eyes and picture this," Lily commanded. All sixteen girls squeezed them shut. "Believe this: We are all Brookville. We are all Bombers, and today . . . we are the champions!"

The girls lifted their arms like a fountain and shouted together, "Champions!"

chapter 20

Both squads took to the field and Lily sprinted down the sidelines. She spied Aunt Dina and her grandfather at the concession stand.

"Dina!" Lily shouted as she rushed over to her aunt. "What are you doing way over here?"

"Oh, Pop Pop needed another hot dog," Dina answered with a sigh. "Boy, LJ, I hope your team can get a goal. Or two."

"We will," Lily said firmly, "but we're going to need your help."

Lily explained what she had in mind and Dina just laughed. "You got it, squirt."

The whistle blew, signaling the start of the second half. Lily turned to go.

"Brutta?" Pop Pop blurted suddenly.

Lily turned around and stared at the old man.

"Hai fame?" he asked, offering his chili dog.

"No, I'm not hungry, but thanks, Pop Pop." Lily laughed. The sharing of food was quite a peace offering. She hugged her grandfather, noting how fragile yet fierce he felt in her arms. Lily smelled something different.

"Pop Pop, are you wearing cologne?" she asked, sniffing the air.

The old man winked and kissed Lily on the cheek. She hugged him again and sprinted back to the bench.

"Where were you?" Chris asked.

"Getting reinforcements."

All the crazy energy of the first half was gone. The Bombers started the second half like they were winning 3–0, not losing 0–1. Vee and Sue were working it up the middle, connecting on passes and trying to break into Castle Creek's eighteen-yard box. It was clear Castle Creek had a simple strategy: hold on to the lead. They had moved two of their strong midfielders into the defense and were crowding the box. Every time the Bombers pushed forward, defenders overwhelmed them. There was just no room to play.

"Work the outsides, girls!" Chris called, trying to create more space behind the defense. Vee responded by sending balls outside to Tabitha on the wing.

"Hold on to it as long as you can, Tabitha," Chris directed. To Lily he said, "If she can draw a few defenders to the outside, maybe we'll have a chance of hitting Vee in the middle."

LJ nodded; she'd been thinking the same thing.

The whistle blew. Reese, the Bombers' midfielder, was booked with a yellow card for tripping after the Castle Creek forward made a move toward the Bomber goal. "Next one's a red, Coach," the ref called to the sidelines.

"Ref, substitution!" Chris called. "Reese, come take a break."

Reese came to the sidelines and sat next to Lily on the bench. "It's getting ugly out there," she said.

"I know you're all getting tired," Chris said. "But you have to keep your head about you. This is no time to start fouling. Castle Creek is just too danger-ous on free kicks."

Molly Barrelton placed the ball down about twenty-five yards out, definitely in a position to prove him right. Beth, the Bombers' goalie, called for a four-person wall. Sue, Tabitha, Amelia and Vee lined up ten yards in front of the ball, creating a human wall between the ball and the goal.

"Back it up," the ref said to the wall. As the girls inched backward, Opera Lady got her second wind.

"Castle *Creek*! Castle *Creek*!" she sang.

Oh no, not again, Lily thought. She searched the sidelines with her eyes.

"Castle *Creek*! Let's do it again, Castle Creek!" Her voice polluted the air like secondhand smoke.

"Darn," Chris muttered under his breath.

As Opera Lady opened her impressive mouth to start another round, a chant began on the other side of the field.

"De-*fense*! De-*fense*!" Aunt Dina shouted at the top of her lungs.

"Castle *Creek*!"

"De-*fense*!" She was standing now, raising her arms to get the Nuts and Berries to join in. "De-*fense*! De-*fense*!"

All the parents responded. BlackBerries and video cameras were down. Every Bomber fan in sight took up the cause. Soon the entire field was staring at the crowd, including Molly, the wall of girls and the referee. The game had come to a complete standstill as the cheering sections had a championship of their own.

Some of the players covered their ears, and the referee's restart whistle was drowned out by the crowd.

"Stooooooop!!" a voice finally cried from the field. "Please! Aunt Bella, just stop!"

It was Molly Barrelton. Aunt Bella's face was red, and sweat ran down the sides of her face. Mercifully, she was silent. Lily thought she looked exhausted. Dina and the Bomber crew gave one last "Defense!" for good measure and then went quiet too.

"Play on!" boomed the referee, and the whistle blew again. All eyes returned to the field as Molly prepared to shoot. Beth got set on her goalie line. This was a do-or-die situation. Molly approached, but something looked off. Her timing was wrong; Lily recognized it at once. Molly wound up having to stutter her steps as she reached the ball and as a result leaned way too far back. The ball went sailing harmlessly over the goal.

The Bombers crowd gave a demure cheer and Lily, Chris and the rest of the bench shared a group exhale and hug.

"How much time left?" Reese asked Chris.

"Two minutes," he answered stonily. "We've got to get a goal. Now."

Beth sprinted behind the goal to retrieve the ball and sent it upfield. It glanced off Amelia's head and there was a mad scramble at midfield. Once again, Molly Barrelton somehow emerged with the ball. Lily was on her feet. It took all her will not to run on the field.

"Stop her!" Lily yelled.

Out of nowhere a blur of blue and yellow swooped in. Vee. She stole the ball from Molly and sent a looping pass over the defense. The ball landed in open field. Castle Creek had moved up for the free kick, and finally there was space behind the defense. The ball was loose. Like a gazelle, Tabitha swooped in and began dribbling toward the goal.

Oh, please don't yell anything stupid, Lily willed as she watched Mr. Gordon jump to his feet. Luckily, he was too shocked to say anything. He and Mark watched with open mouths as Tabitha headed to goal.

The crowd stood.

It was just Tabitha and the goalie.

Breakaway.

The Castle Creek sweeper gave chase. Tabitha crossed into the box, slowed down and raised her head to shoot. The goalie came forward. The sweeper caught up. Tabitha gave one last touch.

The sweeper grabbed at Tabitha's arm. She grabbed her uniform. Tabitha tried to get the shot off, but it was too late: the defender grabbed her from behind and pulled her to the ground. Lily heard a whistle.

Lily jumped up. Was the game over? No! It couldn't end like this! Tabitha was tripped!

"This isn't football, ref!" Chris yelled. "That's a card!"

Lily was surprised to see Mr. Gordon approach the field, point at the ref and yell, "Hey, that's my kid!"

Tabitha slowly got to her feet and shook off the penalty. The referee held up his hand to keep her father off the field, then flashed a red card from his back pocket. The sweeper was ejected from the game. The referee then sprinted over to the little white mark twelve yards from the goal. He pointed to the ground.

"Penalty kick," he said. "Coach, choose your kicker."

The Bombers fans erupted. The Castle Creek crowd booed and berated the referee as a cheater. One mother accused him of taking bribes.

"Vee, you take it," Chris called from the bench. He glanced down at Lily.

Vee picked up the ball and shook her head no.

"Is it your ankle?" Chris called.

Vee shook her head again. She walked over to Tabitha and held out the ball. Before Chris could object, Lily grabbed his arm.

"She can do it," she said.

"Tabitha?"

"Tabitha."

Tabitha looked to the sidelines. Slowly, Chris nodded.

Tabitha placed the ball on the kicker's mark. Lily watched her eyes. She looked only at the ball. Don't look at the goalie, Lily willed. Whatever you do, don't look up.

The sideline was silent. Lily thought Mr. Gordon looked green in the gills, like he was about to throw up. The Bombers gathered together and held hands. The goalie watched Tabitha's every move.

Tabitha took a few steps back.

She stood up straight.

Her eyes were shut tight.

Lily inhaled.

Tabitha kept her eyes closed and lowered her

head. She opened them slowly and looked only at the ball.

The goalie studied her—Tabitha's eyes, her feet, her body posture—but Tabitha gave nothing away.

The whistle blew. Lily was too nervous to exhale.

Tabitha raised herself on her toes ever so slightly and then stepped forward without hesitation. Her eyes and head never moved from the ball.

At the last possible second, she adjusted her foot position.

The ball went low and right. The goalie was caught flat-footed, not knowing which way to lean. When she saw the direction of the shot, she laid her body out and reached as far as she could. Her fingertips brushed the ball. It veered farther right. There was a clang as leather connected with the inside metal post. Then the netting moved with a telltale swoosh.

The referee blew the whistle once and pointed to midfield.

Goal.

Then he blew it again to signal that regulation play was over.

Tabitha leapt like the Sugarplum Fairy as her teammates hugged and shouted in elation and relief. Lily could breathe again.

The game was tied.

The Bombers were still alive.

chapter 21

Overtime.

"One second, ref." Chris ran over to him.

Then LJ's coach handed over a small card. The referee inspected both sides, nodded and handed it back.

"What was that?" she asked as Chris came back to the bench.

"A player card," he answered. "Needed to let him know I was checking in a new player."

Lily's eyes widened.

"LJ, I suspended you for two games."

"Right . . ."

"Well, technically, the second game just ended." Chris smiled.

"I'm back on the team?" she asked. "I can play?"

"Technically, you've never left the team," he told

her. "I can sub you in at any time. That is, if it's okay with your parents."

Lily sprinted toward her mother and father. "Coach says I can play if it's okay with you. Can I?"

Her mother was holding her bag. She reached inside and pulled out a neatly folded blue uniform, shin guards and Lily's cleats.

"I thought you'd want them here," her mother said, smiling. "You know, for moral support."

"Coaches, two minutes to kickoff!" the referee boomed. "You know the rules: Ten minutes of golden goal. First team to score wins. Girls, keep it clean and good luck."

"Ready, LJ?" Chris asked when she was back on the sideline.

Was he kidding?

Lily sprinted to center field. Vee and Tabitha beamed as they took their positions on the front line. Their uniforms were battle-marked with dirt and grass and their faces smudged with mud. The number seven of Lily's clean shirt felt cold and crisp on her back.

Her legs were fresh and her mind clear. Maybe clearer than it had ever been. Here comes the cavalry, she thought. Lily caught her coach's eye and got a thumbs-up in return.

The James family stood huddled together close to the bench while the Nuts and Berries worked the sidelines with the nervous solidarity of shared gray hairs, bitten nails and sore vocal cords. LJ warmed inside when she noticed the intense way Mr. Gordon studied his daughter. His BlackBerry was finally holstered.

At the flick of an elbow, attention narrowed as the referee raised the shiny whistle to his mouth. Lily savored the silence and space before he exhaled. She drank up the expectation and anticipation of all the girls on the field. She looked at Molly Barrelton and the rest of the Castle Creek squad. Champions would be crowned in the next ten minutes, but champions already stood on both sides of this field, she realized.

The whistle blew and Castle Creek kicked off. Lily wasn't in a hurry. She took a minute to get into the flow of the game. After ninety minutes of regulation, players on both sides were tired. Yet there was a rhythm to the way each side was moving, and Lily wanted to pace herself until exactly the right moment. A flash of a white shirt caught her eye, but Lily looked away. Nothing on the sidelines was going to distract her today.

She got her first touch on the ball from a pass from Sue. Lily quickly found an open teammate. Keep the ball moving. Chris's plan was simple: let the ball do the work. Everyone is exhausted, he'd told them, so make good crisp passes and keep control. There was a time, Lily knew, when she'd have just taken the ball and run with it. There was a time not too long ago when she was convinced she didn't need anyone else to win. She thought she could do it all. She got another pass, this time from Tabitha. She two-touched it to Amelia down the line.

"That's it, ladies, work together!" she heard Chris yell.

The Castle Creek defense broke up the next pass and sent a long frantic blooper down the line. The right-winger chased it down, but Lily could see she had nothing left in her legs. Patience, she thought, patience. She covered the field like a tiger stalking prey.

Lily relished the pounding of her cleats on the grass and her heart in her chest. She felt alive again. The Bombers were still on a high from Tabitha's goal, but Castle Creek were the defending champions, and they were determined to hold on to the title. Lily and her teammates couldn't afford to make any mistakes, and they had to capitalize on any and every opportunity.

Molly Barrelton made a run through the offense that caught the tired Bomber defense off guard. Lily was the only one on the team able to give chase. She tracked Molly all the way to the end line and managed to force a goal kick by deflecting the ball out of bounds off Molly's foot.

"Way to get back on defense, LJ!" she heard Chris yell from the sidelines.

Beth launched the ball toward midfield as Lily moved back into the offense. Vee passed it back to

Lily. She moved forward a few yards, then found Reese on the left. She mishandled the trap and lost the ball out of bounds.

"That's okay, Reese!" Lily called. "Next time."

Reese lifted her head and got back in the game. Castle Creek took the throw-in and passed it among the backfield, from one defender to the next. Lily watched as Vee found a burst of energy and put pressure on the outside back, trying to force a mistake. Lily crept forward, looking for an opportunity. She waited and watched as Vee cornered the defender.

The girl began to panic and run back toward her own goal, looking to pass it back to the goalie. Vee stayed on her, herding her deeper into her own territory. Then Tabitha joined the chase. The girl tried to just get rid of the ball by kicking it out of bounds, but it ricocheted off Vee's foot and bounced behind her.

It was the chance Lily was waiting for. Tabitha swooped in and controlled the ball. She passed to Lily, who was open at the top of the box. She looked to pass.

"Go!" Vee cried. "Go to goal!"

Lily looked up. The left fullback was approaching quickly, but if she could beat her, she would be one-on-one with the goalie. With one successful move, she would be home free. Again, time seemed to slow. Lily moved ahead, dribbling with her left foot only. She went straight at the defender. The girl moved forward to tackle, but Lily pushed the ball past her with her left foot and, at the last second, moved her body to the right. The ball shot forward and Lily glided past without any contact.

She exploded onward, pushing her legs to the limit and bringing the ball back under control. She'd done it. It was just Lily, the ball and the goalie. Lily's gait felt light and fast as she burst forward. The goalie came off her line. The din of the crowd grew. Lily slowed down a touch—she was just fifteen yards out. She looked for a shot, but the goalie cut off the angle.

Lily moved closer. The goalie closed in. It was now or never.

The keeper's shirt was a blur of attacking red.

She lunged for the ball. Suddenly a voice called out, "I'm here, LJ!"

Lily took one more touch and then, without even looking up, touched a blind pass out to her right.

The goalie tried to redirect her body to follow the ball, but the pass had caught her off guard. She had been sure Lily would shoot.

The ball rolled gently across the pitch.

Where it met the blur of blue and yellow.

Vee the Bee, of course. Right on schedule.

She approached Lily's pass quickly and confidently but didn't take any chances. Vee dribbled the ball calmly over the white goal line and slammed the game winner into the back of the net.

"Yes!" Lily cried as the whistle blew.

She jumped high into the air.

A sea of crazed teammates arrived and dragged her down into a pile of celebration. Tears, cheers and screams filled her ears as Lily searched for Vee. She found her friend and hugged her tight. Tabitha grabbed them both with a yell as parents and coaches hovered near.

Even Mr. Gordon was applauding.

One by one, each Bomber joined the embrace until they formed a tight circle of smiles. Lily studied every sweaty tired grin. Her friends. Her team.

This was her place in the world. She knew.

Acknowledgments

Lily James is a fictional character, but I must thank my very real and amazing daughter, Lily Jebejian, for the use of her first name and of course for the joy she brings me every day. Also, I again thank the boys of my house, Diron and William Jebejian, the silliest and best crew around. Your love, patience and support are everything.

Special acknowledgment to the many Montalbanos who helped from start to finish: My wonderful mother, Kay, for sharing her love of books and reading and for sticking me on a soccer field as a little girl. My big brother, Dennis, for being my best coach in so many ways. His life, soccer and writing expertise were invaluable. My sister, Teya, for patiently reading every page, often as soon as it was written. Rosanna for checking the Spanish and Italian (any mistakes are my own), and Greg for the website. I am also grateful to Vincent, Patricia, Kelly Berryman, Thomas, Benjamin, Dan, Tiva and Marian Smith for all their endless support and to, of course, the many cheering Jebejians and Kasparians.

Breakaway would never have happened without the amazing Esther Newberg, a one-of-a-kind agent and friend. A special acknowledgment goes to my editor, Philomel's Michael Green, for making every part of the book better. I am eternally grateful for his guidance and for giving me a shot.

Thanks also to Philomel's Tamra Tuller and ICM's Kari Stuart for all their hard work and the million things they do that I never even know about.

Thanks to the dedicated soccer coaches of my life: Chris Moore, Ralph Foster, Joe Massi, Roland Gomez, and Bob Scalise. But in particular, I would like to offer special thanks to Harvard's Tim Wheaton for his knowledge, help and, most important, his friendship. Countless teammates, friends and colleagues encouraged me to write and I am indebted to Carl Hiaasen, Tom Touchet, Meaghan Rady, Elena Patterson, Stacey Vollman Warwick, and Jackie Gross Kellogg. I am grateful to Joanne Jones and Erin Krestinski for the early reads and priceless hours of peace and quiet. A special acknowledgment to Verenice Merino, my Vee, for her steadfast patience and love. Thank you, Nana.

Finally, this book is in many ways a tribute to my late father, William D. Montalbano. Words are not enough, Dad, but thank you.